Echoes of Alice

J. J. Kennard

DEDICATION

To all the believers

CONTENTS

1   Alice   1

2   Anne, Millie & Sam   15

3   Newcomer   19

4   Another Alice   25

5   Visitors   31

6   The Protest   39

7   Alice Drew & Apple Pie   45

8   Changes in the Air   51

9   Anniversary   57

10 Asset Stripping   61

11 Kenny   68

12 Blackmail   73

13 A Secret Shared   79

14 Disclosure   84

15 Another Piece of the Puzzle   90

16 The Fire   95

17 Progress and Impasse   100

18 Harry   105

19 Brad Pitt   109

20 Burnkey Village   114

21 A Message   120

22 Tea and Traces   127

23 The Big Reveal   133

24 Truth Matters   139

1 ALICE

When Alice Ross received her diagnosis, her husband, Dominic, thought his heart had broken. Little did he realise it was just a foretaste of what was to come.

His shock and disbelief was quickly followed by tears and anguished fretful questions. Why? Why her? Why us?

He tried to take charge. He said knowledge was power and so he dealt with his emotions by converting them into action. He began surfing the net, checking obscure databases, subscribing to academic journals. He spent his free time seeking insights and solutions, distracting himself, while Alice sought comfort from her elderly mother.

Days and nights merged.

The life they had known ground to a halt.

Dom's time spent on lengthy thoughtful walks, aimed at stirring his creative juices, were replaced by long hours sitting in hospital corridors and drinking something laughably called coffee.

Alice meanwhile underwent a string of tests.

Ultimately, both Dom and Alice were pragmatists. Not for them alternative therapies, or some trip to a holy man halfway up a mountain. Science and modern medicine was the key and it was where they placed their faith.

That morning, the morning his heart actually broke, he and Alice sat close together, their fingers tightly entwined. They perched on the edge of ash-coloured wooden chairs with green padding, so beloved of clinics and hospitals. They were exhausted from worry and sleepless nights, so they gazed bog-eyed at the empty chair opposite them, waiting for the consultant.

Dom sensed what was coming, but until the words were actually spoken, it still felt like there was a chance.

Even now, Dr Shah could reveal some unexpected medical breakthrough. But when he did appear, his expression said otherwise. Dr Shah was a big man who sat down heavily, and sighed deeply. He didn't beat around the bush. His large brown eyes looked directly at Alice and he said the words they feared.

That was when Dom began to fall apart.

He heard words like, 'aggressive cancer' and 'too late,' and he thought he might be sick. He gulped repeatedly, trying to control his gag reflex. He heard Alice ask 'how long?' Dr Shah answered, 'perhaps a few weeks.'

The room began to turn and it was only when he felt his hand being squeezed insistently, that he became aware of Alice's voice asking him what he thought.

He didn't know what he thought. He could barely comprehend what was happening. He hadn't heard a thing, so he simply nodded, hoping that was enough.

Then, they were outside, looking for a taxi. Alice snuggled up to him, shielding herself from a sharp easterly wind. She complained that it was bitter, but the only bitterness Dom felt was growing inside him. He looked around at people going about their business and wondered what made them so special and worthy of life.

She sensed his disquiet and pulled him along.

They walked to a coffee shop, just around the corner from the hospital. Alice chose a window seat and began passing comments about the display of wigs in the grubby little shop opposite.

'I suppose they get a steady trade from the hospital,' she said. 'All those bald heads from radiation therapy.'

He studied her expression as she gazed out of the window, holding her coffee cup the way she always did, the rim just below her lips. Even now she was trying to hold him together. It was perverse. Alice, ever calm and measured, supporting *his* implosion over the news of her impending death.
She met his frightened gaze and gave him a reassuring smile.

He began to shake. She reached over and cupped his hands in her own. 'Dom, you're trembling.' She studied his face and raised her eyebrows. 'Are you going to throw up?'
He offered up a tight smile. 'I think I'm over that,' he said, 'but Dr Shah came close to having his room redecorated.'
Alice said something about blood-sugar levels and told him to eat his blueberry muffin. As always, he did what she suggested and began to feel better.

When they got home, Dom put the kettle on and made tea. He called out that it was ready but got no response. He went upstairs and found Alice sitting tightly on the edge of the bed, sobbing quietly.
She suddenly looked so small and frail.
'I'd hoped for a little longer, Dom' she sniffed.

He strained to think of something to say, something useful, helpful, reassuring perhaps, but nothing came. He was meant to be a man of words, a writer, but he was spent. And so he sat on the bed next to the only woman he had ever loved. He cradled her in his arms and kissed her head. He stroked her cheek and wiped her tears and rocked her gently, until eventually she fell asleep.

Later that day she began to pack a suitcase and Dom asked what she was doing.
Alice looked up at him with mild exasperation. 'I asked you what you

thought, and you agreed. It's too late to change your mind.' She caught his puzzled expression and filled in the gap by reminding him they'd agreed the best thing was for her to be hospitalised as soon as possible. They could control her symptoms more effectively that way.

Alice was admitted two days later, on her 31st birthday. The medication she'd been taking was already less effective, but they worked a kind of magic with new concoctions.

For days after she remained lucid, pain free, and seemed almost well. But it was an illusion. The weeks Dr Shah had given Alice turned out to be days. She died at 4 a.m. on a drizzly Tuesday morning, with Dominic by her side.

At that moment, he began to die inside.

***

Norfolk roads hadn't improved since Dom last drove on them. Harvest time tractors stubbornly refused to pull aside and there were precious few places to overtake. Alice would have told him to relax and put the radio on, and so he did. It helped of course. He found himself smiling at the fact that she was still telling him what to do.

At first glance, The Old School House looked pretty shabby, but the survey report said any problems were cosmetic. It had been well over a year since he'd seen the place. Alice was born here. She'd spent a happy childhood in this very building. When it came up for sale, her school friend, Anne, who still lived in the village, contacted her. Alice couldn't believe her luck. She and Dom had agreed it was time to stop giving the landlord nearly a third of their income and get a mortgage.

Dom was mentally adrift as usual, halfway into writing a novel and under pressure to meet a deadline. He passed the responsibility for finding a place to her. It never crossed his mind that they might move from Manchester to Norfolk.

'Do they even have Internet in Norfolk?' He grumbled.

'Don't be daft,' she said, and then looked doubtful.

It was all he needed to pull up Google. He rubbed his chin. 'Ah yes, here's a local company offering a free turnip with every sign up, and here,' he pointed to his screen with mock enthusiasm, 'there's one offering to upgrade systems to steam power.'

Alice had that faraway look in her eyes and he knew she was impervious to his cynicism. 'Don't they still get the plague?' he muttered weakly, before finally giving up.

The weeks passed. One night, Dom lifted his hands from the keyboard as though finishing a piano recital. He leaned back, clasped his hands behind his head and said a triumphal, 'yes'.

'Pleased with it?' Alice asked.

He said he thought he'd get away with it for a first draft and his mood lifted. 'Right, let's go out for that curry.'

Alice was curled up on the sofa, reading a magazine. She raised an eyebrow. 'At midnight, on a Sunday?'

He looked at his watch. 'Is it?'

Alice pursed her lips and flicked a couple of pages. 'Doesn't matter. Anyway, a little self-care is in order, plus you're practically sitting on your golden locks.'

The memory made him run his fingers through his hair. It was thick and luxuriant. It grew at an alarming rate and flopped over his face. It was nearly always longer than Alice liked, but it seemed to turn the heads of women and men alike.

He was tall and slim and he knew he was attractive to women, not that he'd capitalised on it. Alice said he had a public schoolboy look, whatever that meant. But once, during a passionate clinch, she described him as her Nordic God. It was over-the-top of course, but he liked it.

He stood by the entrance to the Old School House and felt relief. 'Here we are, Alice,' he muttered. 'We've got it. Everything you wanted.'

The winding pathway was partially blocked by a rickety wooden gate that had rotted off its hinges. Dom spent a few moments studying the support pillar until he found what he was looking for. Alice's initials, A.P. crudely carved into the wood. Her maiden name was Peters.
He touched the letters and closed his eyes, willing a connection to her, imagining her as a child scratching away with a penknife.

He stood up, pushed the gate to one side and walked a few paces along the hedge-lined drive. A gentle breeze had picked up, causing the leaves to twinkle and rustle. From somewhere nearby a frog croaked. A dragonfly hovered for a moment, the afternoon sunlight glinting off its frantic, fragile wings. It was easy to see why Alice found magic here.

Dom side-stepped onto the overgrown lawn in order to get a clearer view of the house. It was a decent size and a sturdy looking place. Two, tall windows, dominated the ground floor and four smaller ran along the length of the first floor. He took out his mobile phone and checked the compass app. The front of the house would catch the morning sun, facing east. He made a mental note to sleep in one of the front bedrooms.

He skirted around the garden. To the south, a large chimneystack, with four pots, dominated the side of the house. A honeysuckle draped potting shed, stood next to a line of abandoned beehives. At the back of the house, a stone-slab patio was almost overrun with brambles. Trees and mixed hedging defined the boundary. A modern looking barn came with the house. It crossed his mind he could use it for storage.
He returned to the front and pulled out a bunch of keys. He guessed the biggest of them fitted the stout old door with its deep inset lock. He was right.

Inside, it felt warm and inviting. The door narrow doorway opened directly into a large central room that he guessed was once the classroom. Flecks of dust hung in molten-gold shafts of sunlight. It had the comforting smell of an old bookshop.

The kitchen was smaller than he'd been used to, but more than enough
for a microwave, toaster and kettle. The cupboards were old but
serviceable and there was the obvious gap for a washing machine.
He returned to the main room and climbed the stairs, offset to one side.
They creaked loudly and he made a mental note to get them sorted out.
The three bedrooms were roughly similar sizes, although the one he'd
designated as his own was marginally bigger. The two at the back
looked over fields and the Broads. A couple of pleasure cruisers in the
distance provided the only signs of human life.

His bedroom looked over the edge of the village. It was a chocolate box
view. A hedge-lined ancient track, meandered towards a church and the
shell of a windmill. He reached up and touched the stout oak beam
above his head. It had some signs of charring. Horse brasses were nailed
into the timber. They would have to go, it reminded him too much of a
pub. The thought of the pub made his stomach rumble.

It was a ten-minute walk to the *The Bomber*. Inside, a handful of people
sat at tables or propped up the bar. Dom ordered a pint of the local
bitter and settled on cod and chips, chalked on the board as meal of the
day.
The walls were adorned with old photographs of bomber crews who
were stationed nearby during the war. It was strange to imagine them
standing on this very spot, drinking what might have been their last
glass of warm beer.

'On holiday, are you?'
He turned in the direction of the voice. It belonged to a woman about
his age. She was dressed in a blue boiler suit and green wellington boots
and was checking him out. He could see that she had long red hair
stuffed beneath a black beret. She smiled, revealing a generous row of
large white teeth.

He took a sip of beer and made an effort to be polite. 'I've just moved into the Old School House.'

'Really?' she said, surprised. Realisation dawned. 'You're Dominic, aren't you? I thought you looked familiar.'

He studied her face for a moment, then made the connection. 'Oh, it's Anne, isn't it? You were at Alice's . .' he found he was unable to say the last word.

Anne's smile collapsed as she saw the pain etched on Dominic's face. 'It was a lovely service,' she said self-consciously.

It had been a while since anyone had spoken about Alice and his emotions were still raw. He gave Anne a barely noticeable nod of acknowledgement and moved away to find a table.
Anne looked crestfallen. She turned back the bar, necked the remains of her drink and turned to leave.
Dom looked up as she went out the door. At some level he knew he should feel more contrite, but in truth he didn't care.

As he stared into the depths of his drink he could sense Alice giving him an earful. *You prick! That's one of my oldest friends you've just snubbed.* But then his meal arrived and, for a time, even Alice was moved to the background.

It was getting dark when he made it back to the house. He dragged a couple of suitcases from the boot of his aging Volvo and stuffed a sleeping bag under his arm.

There followed a brief moment of concern. He couldn't recall checking whether the mains services had been switched on. He flicked the light switch and was relieved to see a sharp glow from a single bulb fill the space.

Dom walked through the entrance, dropped his cases and dragged the sleeping bag up the stairs, which snapped and creaked beneath his weight. Back downstairs he unzipped one of the cases and pulled out a kettle and jar of instant coffee. He turned the kitchen tap, which grunted and spat into life. Everything a man could need, he thought.

It wasn't late, but he was tired and felt ready for bed. He flicked the clips of the second suitcase and removed two framed photographs. One was of Alice, holding a daffodil above her head. The other, his favourite, was of them cuddling on some airport waiting lounge during a flight delay. It was early in their relationship and they radiated love. He ran the tip of his finger down her face and felt his throat tighten. He could sense her saying, *don't be maudlin. You get like this when you've had a few and it isn't pretty.*

A knock at the door interrupted his reverie. Dom looked out of the window and saw a white van. His furniture wasn't meant to arrive until the following day, but maybe this was some kind of advance party?

He opened the door to three middle-aged men. One was hauling equipment out of the van, another hung back from the door looking uncertain, but the one he took to be the leader thrust his hand forward. Dom found himself on automatic pilot and shook it.

'That's a relief,' said the stranger. 'We got wind of the fact someone was moving in tomorrow, so we thought we'd grab the chance. I'm Harry Wells, that's Tom,' he thumbed to the man standing behind him who offered up a nervous smile, 'and the one doing the heavy lifting is Dick Thornberry.'

Dom looked towards the van and realised he didn't recognise any of the stuff being pulled out. 'Are you the removals people, he asked?' Then the penny dropped. 'Wait a minute, Tom, Dick and Harry,' he thrust his hands on his hips, 'yes, very funny, so who put you up to this?'

Harry Wells frowned and looked over his shoulder for some support. Tom, standing behind him, found a reason to check his phone. Dick, by the van, stopped moving equipment and stood with his back to them.

'No,' Harry replied hesitantly, 'we're from the NPS, didn't the estate agent tell you about us?'

'NPS?'

'Norfolk Paranormal Society,' Harry said, 'here for a final sweep.' Seeing Dom's jaw start to loosen he pressed on. 'We were here once before and got a couple of interesting readings. We like to put some time between first and subsequent readings as a way of triangulating our findings.'

'You're ghost hunters,' Dom groaned. He rolled his eyes, wondering what he'd done to deserve this.

Harry tipped his head to one side and looked hurt. 'If you like,' he said, 'although the term ghost isn't one members of the Society like to use. You see, paranormal activity can take many different forms and . .'

Dom held a hand up to silence him. 'Look, I'm sure it's all very interesting but I'm just not in the mood. It's been a long day, so goodbye.'

He began to close the door.

'We've travelled a long way,' Harry said desperately, 'won't you at least let me explain what we hope to do?'

In the time it took to half close the door, Dom was already a step ahead. It was a long shot and it went against everything he believed, but if there was just a chance these characters could find some link to Alice, he'd take it. The worst that could happen is that he'd look an idiot, but who would even notice when he was surrounded by them. He pulled the door open. 'How long?'

Harry perked up. 'Well, normally we'd like to spend the night, but given your circumstances, say a couple of hours? Three maybe?' He rubbed his hands in anticipation.

Dom checked his watch. 'Here's the deal. Do your thing and be out of here in three hours, tops.' He saw the disappointment on Harry's face but he wasn't in the mood for compromise.

Harry agreed.

Dom stepped aside as they rushed their equipment into the main room and began to set up. Harry gave a running commentary, explaining that the vast majority of creaks and bumps in the night could easily be put down to natural phenomena. 'Central heating pipes, wind, birds up the chimney, we've seen it all.'

Dom took himself into the kitchen and put the kettle on. He only had a couple of mugs but figured they could share.

Harry caught up with him in the kitchen. 'We're going silent now,' he said. 'Actually it's more very quiet, but it helps us rule out extraneous interference.' He looked at the coffee. 'But we're all up for a coffee.'

Dom pulled a face but didn't comment. He was already regretting letting them in and felt a renewed urge to go to bed. He poured water into one of the mugs then decided, as it was his house and his coffee, he'd have the first drink. He didn't really want it and so after a minute he poured it away, rinsed the mug and made another.

He joined the others, coffees in hand. As he entered the main room, the one called Tom lifted a finger to his lips and pointed, what looked like a microphone, in Dom's direction.

Dom remained still while Tom checked readings on a pack strapped to his waist. Satisfied, Tom moved on, checking the walls.

Further in the room, Harry was doing something with a laptop, while Dick and a young woman Dom hadn't previously noticed, stared intently at a monitor.

Dom crept forward with the coffee.

Dick looked up, smiled and pointed to a space next to him.

Dom offered the next to the young woman. She looked at him quizzically then turned to look behind her. When she turned back, she pointed to herself, questioningly. He gestured with his head where he'd put her coffee. Open-mouthed and wide-eyed she gave a nod. Dom thought she was gormless.

He retreated to the kitchen, closed the door and nuked a pot-noodle in the microwave. When it was done he opened the back door and stepped into the night. It was a cloudless sky and the stars shone with an intensity he'd never seen in the city. He thought he might miss Manchester, but so far, so good. It was early days however and his main concern was the lack of distraction.

Dom lived an ambivalent life. He couldn't leave Alice behind, because he didn't want to. If anything he wanted to be closer, and therein lay a problem. He also knew that without distraction the weight of his grief could overwhelm him. He'd come perilously close to falling apart at the seams a couple of times and he was astute enough to realise that further isolation could very well be the undoing of him.

He felt a presence and turned to see the woman looking back at him wide-eyed. 'Hello.'
She smiled.
'Have you Finished?'

An awkward silence fell between them. She was a strange little thing, Dom thought. She looked the sort who raided charity shops and dressed in gear belonging to a different era. Her high-necked blouse looked positively Victorian and she wore a floor length navy skirt and wide black belt around her waist. Her hair was gathered up into a loose knot and tied with a ribbon.
'Would you like some?' Dom asked, holding up his noodles.
She looked at the noodles and walked back into the house.
That's taking *going silent* to extremes, Dom thought.

He finished his noodles and crept back to the main room.
The men were still focused on their silent activities. He leaned against the wall and noticed the girl was missing. He thought little of it until he saw her walk down the stairs. He wasn't best pleased. He hadn't given them free run of the house. Then he checked himself. It didn't matter - the place was empty.

She stood primly at the end of the room, looking up and down its length. He tried to work out her role in the activities. She didn't use equipment like the others and there was something else niggling away at him, but he couldn't quite put his finger on it.

Dom took himself to a corner and sat on the floor. He only realised he'd fallen asleep when Harry announced it was time to call a halt. Dom blinked himself awake and stood up. 'Anything?' he asked.

Harry shook his head. 'Not this time. It's what we expect really, but it's always worth a second look.'
It was Dom's turn to shake his head. What had he seriously been expecting? Did he honestly think Alice would leave some kind of message via Tom, Dick and Harry? He began laughing at his own stupidity.
'Something funny?' Harry asked.
Dom stared at the floor and took a long deep breath. 'Just a passing thought,' he sighed. 'Can I give you a hand with your gear?'

Harry cast a wary glance in Dom's direction. He thanked him, but said they preferred to pack their own stuff, as they knew where everything went.
To Dom's relief it took much less time to pack away than it did to set up. He stood at the front door while the men put the last of the stuff in their van. 'Well, don't take this the wrong way,' Dom said, 'but no need to rush back.'
Harry understood the slight well enough but he chose to be gracious. 'Thanks again for putting up with us, I'm sorry we took you by surprise.'
'It was,' Dom searched for a word and settled on 'illuminating.' He raised a hand. 'Good to meet the four of you.' As he closed the door he heard one of them say *eh?*

Dom turned off the downstairs light and began to climb the stairs. He was half way up when he realised what had perplexed him earlier.

The girl. When she came down the stairs he heard nothing, yet there wasn't a step that didn't complain beneath his weight. Maybe that's it, he thought, her weight. He remembered her slight build, then shrugged it off and made his way to bed.

2 ANNE, MILLIE AND SAM

Anne Sullivan had just finished milking her small herd of Jersey cows and was spraying down the yard. The snub by Dominic Ross played on her mind and it still stung. She blamed herself for being so crass, but she also blamed him for his arrogance.

Well over a year had passed since Alice died. She could understand how it still hurt, but that didn't excuse bad manners. Anyway, she thought, Dom Ross had always been a bit up himself, plus she'd tried reading one of his books, which she thought was crap, mainly because she couldn't understand it.

She turned around at the sound of Millie running towards her. 'Are you ready for school, honey-bun?'

Millie nodded and asked again when Crunchy was having her baby.

Anne said very soon, but Millie was impatient and wanted to know if it would happen before her birthday, or even better, on her birthday. 'Can I have the baby cow as a birthday present?'

Anne turned off the hose and dropped it next to where she stood. She picked up her five-year-old and gave her a big hug. 'You can certainly give it a name,' Anne said.

She put Millie down and gently guided her back to the house.

Millie complained that she'd already named Crunchy and now she wanted a different present. 'I think you'll get enough presents without needing a cow,' Anne said, 'and anyway, what if it did a poo in the house?'

Millie pinched her nose and started to giggle. It was infectious and so the pair of them pinched their noses and made the sound of a cow, swapping moo for poo noises.

It was a mild, sunny morning and so they walked the half-mile to school. Millie held Anne's hand and sang some songs they were rehearsing at school. As soon as Millie saw her friends she pulled away and gave Anne a quick wave.

Anne stood for a moment watching her daughter chasing and being chased. A couple of the other mums were doing the same and they shared a knowing smile.

She checked her watched and figured that young Terry would have arrived at the farm. He was only 17 but he was solid, reliable and hard working. An added bonus was that he didn't want much money because his dad said the experience would be useful.

Anne crossed the road and made her way to the library.

A fluorescent yellow sheet of A4 was taped to the window calling for people to *Save our Library!*

Anne rummaged about in her shoulder bag. It was big and deep and seemed to contain half her life. She found the book and placed it on the counter.

Samantha Wilson, the librarian, appeared from behind a shelf and pretended to look shocked.

'Hi Sam,' Anne said breezily, 'I said I'd get it back to you and here it is.'

Sam adjusted her spectacles and flipped open the cover to check the date. 'You do realise the printing press had only just been invented when this was due back.'

'Oh no, really? Go on then, hit me with the bill.'

Sam made a show of calculating and announced the fine came to £15.30.

'Oh hell, really!' Anne frowned deeply as she opened her purse, wondering if she had the cash.

Sam looked around to see if anyone was in earshot. 'Oh you pathetic, struggling, single working mother,' she mocked, 'just give me a couple of quid and we'll call it quits.'

Anne made a noise between her lips and slid a coin towards her friend. 'Wish they were all like you, Sweetie.'
'If they were all like me this place would have closed years ago.'
Anne looked around at the near empty building. 'How goes the petition?'
Sam pulled a clipboard from beneath the counter. 'Have you signed?'
'Weeks ago.'
'Has Millie?'
'She's five!'
'Does she use our services?'
'You know she does.'
'Well you can sign on her behalf.'
'Is that legal?'
'Who cares? Anyway, sign, or pay me the other thirteen quid you owe.'
'That's extortion,' Anne said smiling and picking up the pen. 'I've a good mind to report you to the local constabulary.'
Sam tipped her head to one side. 'I like a man in a uniform.' She raised a single eyebrow and replaced the petition.
'Seriously,' Anne said, 'do you think the petition will do any good.'
'Nope. When it comes to cutbacks I think the decision was made months ago. But we can't just roll over and make it easy for them.'

Anne couldn't remember a time when the library hadn't served the village. With the exception of the pub, and maybe the church hall, everything happened here.
But the village was losing ground to places like Norwich, where people could get jobs. Young families were moving out and even the school was under threat.
The place was becoming a holding ground for those of a certain age who resented change. If they weren't careful their cherished village would slowly die. She and Sam often said, remove the life-blood and it's just a

matter of time before the place is flattened for a car park, or bulldozed to make way for an industrial estate.

Sam moved the conversation on. 'Met the incomers yet?'
'Incomer,' Anne corrected. I know him, sort of.' She felt her jaw tighten and wondered if it showed.
Sam was too interested to notice and wanted more information.
Anne told her what she knew about Alice and Dominic Ross.
Sam was intrigued. She said it felt a bit creepy that Dom had moved in to the house where his wife spent her childhood.
Anne filled in the details of her last conversations with Alice, and how excited she'd been that the house was on the market. 'I suppose they snapped it up before, you know, and that's why he's here.'
They paused for a moment, lost in their own thoughts. A lady approached the counter and Sam stamped her book. It signalled a change of mood.

'What can I get Millie for her birthday?' Sam asked.
'She wants a cow, but failing that, a book of night-time stories might be good.'
'Got you covered,' Sam said, gesturing to the children's section.

They said their goodbyes and Anne set off to grab some party snacks from the local shop. Money was tight, as always, but Millie's party was going to go well, so there would be no stinting on food.

3 NEWCOMER

The removals van arrived bang on schedule. Dom threw open the door and let the men get on with it. Most of the furniture remained downstairs. His writing table and chair went in one of the back bedrooms while the third bedroom acted as a storeroom for boxes yet to be unpacked. In just over an hour and they were done. Dom pressed a tip in their hands and pointed in the direction of the pub.

He stood in the middle of the large lounge and looked around. This will do nicely, he thought. Alice would have loved it. He tried to imagine how she might organise the room and decided he would attempt to fulfil those wishes. She would want flowers about the place. He would see to those later.

He went upstairs to his designated study and began to organise it. Boxes of books would have to stay where they were until he could sort out shelving. He located his printer and an extension lead and began positioning things the way he liked them.

He sat at the table. The printer went to his left, the computer in the middle of course, and his favourite photograph of Alice, to his right. As always, he stopped for a few moments to look at her face but his attention was quickly drawn to a movement in the back garden. At first, he thought it was one of the removals men, but then he recognised her as the girl from the ghost club. What the hell was she doing, sniffing around the place?

By the time he got downstairs and into the garden she'd gone. He found he wasn't too bothered. She looked the sort that could burst into tears if the wind changed direction, and that was something he could do without. He went back inside, put the kettle on and made himself a coffee.

In the lounge, he dragged the sofa to a position that allowed him to look over the front garden. He stopped for a moment, wondering if that was what Alice would have done. Probably, yes. She loved looking at wildlife in the garden and this was perfectly positioned. Satisfied, he slumped down. He was just about to take a sip of coffee when he saw the woman at the top of the stairs. At first he couldn't process the audacity of it. He sat dumbstruck and wide-eyed. By the time he found his voice the best he could muster was, 'hey, who said?' But she'd walked away.

Newly invigorated, he put down his coffee mug and ran up the stairs, taking them two at a time. He called out, 'what do think you're doing? There was no answer. He checked his study, then the bathroom and the other bedrooms. Where the hell was she?

He looked above for a loft hatch but couldn't see one. He called out again but was met by silence. He felt perplexed and a bit freaked out. Nobody simply disappears through a brick wall.

He stood in the passageway and tried to focus his thinking. If she had been hiding in his bedroom all she had to do was slip out while he was checking the other rooms and she'd have got away. That must be it, he concluded.

He wouldn't have heard her on the stairs because she wasn't heavy enough. His lips tightened with irritation. What was the name of that ghost place? He'd give them a piece of his mind. There couldn't be that many in Norfolk. He was just about to search for them online when he realized the telephone engineer wasn't due until that afternoon.

Still muttering to himself he went back downstairs. For peace of mind he went around the place one more time, shutting doors and locking those he could. Satisfied, he went back to the business of unpacking.

After a time, he was back in the pub, ordering a beer and a ploughman's lunch. The place was almost empty and the slow pace at which the barman operated gave the impression this was about as busy as it got. He wondered how long a place like this could survive.

He ate his meal and checked his watch. The telephone engineer still wouldn't arrive for another couple of hours, so he had time to stock up on a few provisions.

It didn't take long to work out the shop: two isles, a fridge and a small selection of newspapers and magazines. Dom grabbed bread, eggs, milk and bacon and pondered over the small selection of biscuits. He was vaguely aware of someone standing nearby.

'You look like a lemon puff person to me,' said Anne. She caught his sour expression and immediately regretted opening her mouth. This guy really didn't want human contact. She took a step back, feigned interest in some washing up liquid, and turned away.

'And you look like you've got a sugar habit,' Dom replied.

She looked up to see him staring at her bulging basket of sweets and cakes. Okay, she thought, he's made an effort. He made eye contact for a moment and pulled his mouth in what could have been an apologetic smile. 'My daughter's birthday,' Anne said, 'she'll be six this Saturday.'

Dom nodded and muttered 'happy birthday.' He turned his attention once more to the biscuits and picked up a pack of digestives.

What was it about this guy, Anne wondered? He seemed to have a knack of wrong-footing her even though she'd only ever tried to be friendly. As he started to move away she felt her anger build. She said, 'should I take this personally, or is this surly, want-to-be-alone routine, for everyone?'

Their eyes met in a moment of shared hostility. He chose not to answer and turned away.
'Oh nice,' Anne said, 'that's all the village needs.'
He stopped for a moment, his back to her. 'Meaning?' he asked.
'Meaning some irascible loner who doesn't give a toss about anyone or anything except himself.'

Her comment was met by silence. She couldn't see his face but she watched in horror as his head tilted forwards and his shoulders began to shake.

For a terrible moment she thought she'd made him cry. She intuitively reached forward to touch his shoulder. The words rushed out. 'Look, I'm sorry. I had no right to say that. My big mouth has a life of its own.'

He turned to face her and his expression had the afterglow of someone who had just stopped laughing.

She was surprised, not just by the turn of events, but also the way his demeanour had transformed. The frog had just become prince charming. She found herself pulling a strand of hair over her ear and returning his smile. This was a truly weird person. Good looking, but bonkers.

'Don't apologise,' he said. 'I had it coming.'

She decided not to make it easy for him. She put her heavy basket down and folded her arms defensively. 'You find it funny when people tear a strip off you?'

He studied her as though she'd registered on his radar for the first time. 'It reminded me of someone,' he said.

Anne raised her eyebrows at him and picked up her basket. 'Takes all sorts I suppose.'

As he gazed at her she suddenly saw a different man. He looked lonely and vulnerable. Perhaps he simply didn't want to be hurt any more, or maybe he wanted to make contact but had forgotten how. On impulse she said, 'you're welcome to drop by at Millie's party, this Saturday afternoon. A few people from the village will be there. Chance to mix and mingle - and all that.'

His lingering gaze was starting to unsettle her. 'See you there, maybe.' She headed for the till, puzzled by the encounter.

***

Hello world, Dom thought, as he got back online. He checked his email. Most messages were from his literary agent, pleading, cajoling or threatening him over his lack of progress.

Reality was beginning to bite. Money was running out, bills were piling up, yet motivation was at rock bottom. He really did need to focus and his excuses were wearing thin.

He couldn't blame his surroundings. This place was ideal. He'd purchased it outright from the proceeds of Alice's life insurance. It was quiet and had the kind of ambience most writers would give a kidney for. But his head wasn't in the right place. He grabbed a book and started to read. Reading other people's stuff often stimulated his juices, but not today. After just fifteen minutes he put the book down and began drumming his fingers on the table.

He remembered the ghost hunters. If they turned up again it would definitely disrupt his thought processes. At some level he knew he was only making excuses, but it gave him something to do. A quick search and he pulled up their website. It was an amateurish thing with a layout that had gone out of fashion years earlier. He searched for the contact details and found pictures of Tom, Dick and Harry. They'd obviously taken it in turns with the camera, each of them with the same background. Harry had put some weight on since these were taken, Dom noted. The girl wasn't there. Maybe she'd hooked up with them more recently. He punched the number into his phone and waited. It went to a message service so he gave up.

Some other time then, he thought.

4 ANOTHER ALICE

Screams of delight filled the air as children bounced up and down on the inflatable castle. Most of the food had been ignored although there was quite a dent in the bowls of sweets. Anne found herself worrying about tummy aches and sickness as she watched the kids throw themselves around.

She heard a tap on the window and looked up. Sam Wilson had taken time away from library duties to help out. She held up a box of matches, wondering whether it was time to bring out the cake.

As Anne nodded, Sam pointed to a place where the cars where parked. Anne watched as an old Volvo took its place alongside the line of Land Rover's and assorted SUVs. She could hardly believe it when Dominic Ross stepped out and gave her a wave.

'Is that him?' Sam said breathlessly. She had forgotten about the cake and joined her friend. 'What a hunk.'

Anne gave Sam a playful nudge. 'Don't expect too much, he's a bit prickly.' She interrupted Sam's thought process. 'I know, I know, you like a bit of prickly.' They snorted with laughter at the innuendo. By the time Dom drew closer they managed some restraint and Anne converted her grin into a welcoming smile.

'Here you are,' Dom said self-consciously.

A thought struck Anne. 'Oh heck, I didn't tell you where we lived, did I?'

'Wasn't hard,' Dom said. 'I just asked at the shop if they knew where the party was.'

Millie saw the strange man and had crossed the field to join her mother. She clung to Anne's leg, half hiding.
Dom's expression remained impassive. He looked at Millie, who gazed back at him wide-eyed. 'You must be the birthday girl?'
She nodded shyly as Anne reached down and stroked her hair.
Anne said: 'I have to say, I'm surprised you came.'
Dom smiled, but kept his eyes on Millie. He reached inside his jacket. 'Bet you can't guess what's in here?
Millie stared at what he was doing and shook her head.
Dom straightened up. 'I'll give you one guess,' he said. 'Get it right and you can have it.'
Millie said: 'is it a birthday present?'
A loud *parping* noise came from inside his jacket and, with a flourish, he produced a clown's horn.
Millie squealed with pleasure at the funny noise and told him to do it again, which he did. He passed it to her and said happy birthday.
She ran off squeezing the bulb, the horn getting noisier each time.

Anne grimaced playfully and put her fingertips against her temples, 'remind me never to invite you to anything, ever again,' she said.
As Dom raised his hands in mock supplication, she felt her ankle being tapped. She ran with it. 'Oh, Dominic, this is my friend Samantha,' she looked down at her friend who was pushing her chest out. 'Sam's our librarian and local historian.'

'I also light birthday candles,' Sam grinned cheekily. 'It's a heavy cake, so if you don't mind humping things, I could use your muscles.'
Dom shrugged. 'Sure.'
Anne stifled a smile and rolled her eyes.

As Sam and Dom headed towards the kitchen she began clapping her hands to round the children up. They stood around the table and sang *Happy Birthday*. Millie blew out the candles in one go and followed up with a loud *parp* on her clown's horn.

'I hate you,' Anne muttered in Dom's direction. She wasn't sure he heard as he was trying to extricate himself from Sam's endless chatter and innuendo's.

Parents slowly began to peel away, leaving just a handful of Millie's closest friends. Dom had moved away and was talking to Anne's helper, Terry.
Anne sat next to Sam, who was sampling the birthday cake. 'You do know you're shameless,' Anne said. Sam used her finger to scoop up some buttercream and slowly licked it off.
'For goodness sake,' Anne gasped, 'there are children here.'
Sam covered her mouth with her fingertips and said 'oops.'
Then, as Anne shook her head in exasperation, Sam said, 'the oldest is six. I think we're safe for the time being.'

As Anne helped herself to a paper cup of orange squash, Sam asked what she thought of Dom.
Anne shrugged and said she was amazed he was even here.
Sam accused her of being evasive, so Anne turned the tables and asked what she thought. Sam smirked and said he was welcome to ravage her at a time of his choosing.
Anne pulled a face and wondered why she even bothered to ask.

Dom began to saunter back to where a small group of them were sitting. He looked hesitant, Anne thought. She figured he'd done enough by turning up and didn't see any need to inflict the inevitable string of questions in waiting. She stood up and walked towards him. 'Thanks for stopping by,' she said.

Dom stuffed his hands into his trouser pockets and nodded in acknowledgement. 'Actually,' he said, 'I wanted to ask you something. I wondered if you'd care to join me for a house warming?'
'A party!' Anne stroked her chin. 'You've really taken this community thing to heart.'

He smiled bashfully and she found herself warming to him. 'Tell me when, and I'll organise a baby-sitter.'

'Next Saturday any good?'

The fact that he'd asked a question took her by surprise. 'Am I the first person you've asked?'

'Actually, you're the only person. In fact, it's a party of one, unless you include me.'

She didn't know what to say. In the pause that followed he began to look uncomfortable. 'You don't have to decide now,' he said, 'just give me a call, or text me, if you're free.' He pulled out his wallet and handed her a card. 'I had a hundred of these printed three years ago,' he said, 'you must be the fifth person I've managed to give one to.' He began walking in the direction of his car. 'Great party. Thanks for the invite.'

She looked down at the card. It read, *Dominic Ross, Author,* and contained his email address and mobile phone number. When she looked up he was getting in his car.

***

There was one message waiting for Dom on his return. The voice announced itself as Harry Wells from the NPS, returning his call. Dom was feeling energised and had already pushed the idea of contacting the ghost hunters aside. If Anne accepted his invitation, he could learn so much more about Alice when she was young. Anne would have lots of stories to share. He couldn't wait. He'd have to get some wine in. It would help Anne to relax and she'd be more talkative. He wasn't sure about food. He'd cross that bridge if she accepted his invitation, as he was sure she would. He'd made the effort to go to the party, so she would feel duty bound to reciprocate. He felt pleased with himself. It was a masterstroke of strategic thinking.

He picked up the photograph of Alice and kissed it. As he replaced it, the sound of piano music drifted up the stairs. He stiffened. This had to stop. He cursed himself for not having had the sense to lock the door. He looked downstairs and sure enough, there she was, casually tinkling away on the ivories of Alice's old piano and looking out of the window.

'Excuse me,' Dom called. 'I think you owe me an explanation.'
She looked up at him through distant, dreamy eyes.
'Enough of the silent treatment,' he sputtered, 'I just happen to *live* here, what's your excuse?'
She stopped playing and folded her hands on her lap.

Dom reached the bottom of the stairs. He could feel his heart rate increasing. Jabbing a finger in her direction, he demanded to know what right she had trespassing in his property.
She lifted her chin haughtily.
That movement stopped Dom in his tracks. He looked at the woman warily. The thought she might be mentally ill was beginning to take shape. He decided it could be in both their interests if he became less confrontational.
Then she smiled and perched on the arm of a nearby chair. She wagged a finger at him, as if he was behaving like a naughty boy.

Dom stood with his back pressed against the wall, not quite believing his own eyes. He scowled at her threateningly.
She ignored him and closed her eyes.
Nothing she was doing seemed to make sense. It was as if she was out of phase with her surroundings. Whatever her problem was Dom had had enough. He reached into his pocket and held up his mobile phone. 'You've had your chance,' he said, 'now, I'm calling the police.' He tapped in a number but when he looked up, she was gone.

This time it felt different. He knew there was no point looking around. Instead, he felt goose bumps on his forearms, and a chill down the back of his neck. A thought crossed his mind. Was it possible? He shook his head, trying to displace ridiculous thinking.

He went back upstairs and logged onto his computer. He found the website of the ghost hunters and navigated to the list of projects they had been involved with.

He found the Old School House. The information was sketchy, but something made his skin tingle as he read; *said to be haunted by the ghost of Alice Drew, a former teacher at the school.* A table of data points and graphs showed the results of a previous visit. It meant nothing to him. He felt pretty sure if they were significant, other people would have taken notice.

Dom wondered what to do. If he phoned Tom, Dick and Harry they would inevitably return with all their equipment and he'd never get rid of them. They might inform the press. People would say it was a self-promotion gimmick, a clumsy way of getting some books shifted. It could backfire badly. But, the last time they were here, so was the girl. He remembered when they left, he'd said it was nice meeting the *four* of them. One of them made a noise like they hadn't understood. Did they think he couldn't count, or didn't they see her? He'd seen her easily enough. He'd even seen her in the garden, in broad daylight.

If by any chance she was a ghost, weren't they meant to float about in the dark? Weren't they meant to be translucent?
He slumped back in his chair trying to think. It went against everything he believed, but he didn't care. This could be potential contact with Alice, embarrassment was the least of his worries.

He went downstairs and stood in the middle of the room. 'Hello,' he called out, 'I think I understand now. Will you show yourself to me?' He turned slowly around and then said, 'please.'

Then he asked again, but she did not appear.

5 VISITORS

Sam and Anne sipped their coffee contemplatively. Sam was the first to speak. She asked Anne what she was going to do. Anne didn't know. Sam took a bite of her croissant and spoke through it. She said it was high time for Anne to get back on the dating scene.

'You think it's a date?'

'Of course it's a date.'

'I hardly know him.'

'That's what dates are for. To get to know one another.'

The conversation lapsed as they sipped coffee. Anne then said, 'don't you think he's a bit, well, odd?'

'No. But you are. You're questioning why a highly desirable widower asks a single mother, who spends her days in Wellies, and smells of cow incidentally, out for a drink.' She paused to reflect. 'Actually that is a bit odd.'

'Good point though,' Anne said. 'There's the babysitter to consider, plus I have to be up at the crack of dawn, so he wouldn't expect me to stay out late.'

'Or stay overnight, perish the thought,' Sam groaned.

Anne shifted uncomfortably in her seat. 'I don't see him that way, Sam.'

Sam pulled a face, suggesting she knew otherwise. She nudged the topic forward. 'So, what will you wear?'

'Who says I'm going?'

The questions and answers batted back and forth for another twenty minutes. Anne eventually said she would go, but only out of politeness. She would also make it clear that she could only stay for a couple of hours. After all, sleep would be needed and cows had to be milked. As for clothing, Anne was all for jeans and a jersey.
Sam got frustrated and said the least Anne could do was make an effort. She was certain that Dom was the type who would be really well turned out.
Anne reluctantly bowed to Sam's insights in such matters. She'd had more men than it was decent to count.
'Should I take a bottle?' Anne asked anxiously.
Sam looked as if she had been asked the dumbest question ever. She leaned into the table and whispered, 'yes dear, but not milk.'

Anne phoned Dom when she got home. She thanked him for the invitation and said she'd like to come. She said it was only fair to mention that she'd have to leave early and explained why. She felt a frisson of anticipation when he said he couldn't wait to see her.

When Saturday arrived, she tried on her three dresses, three times, before settling for the black one. As for shoes, she couldn't believe they had ever fitted. She opted for the least painful pair, thinking she could always kick them off later. She played around with her hair. It was a shoulder length mass of copper-red curls that did what it wanted and so she quickly gave up. False eyelashes, she thought, were a step too far. Kenny King, her estranged lover and father of Millie, said her emerald green eyes did all the talking. She always thought it was a stupid thing to say because eyes don't talk; but then Kenny was never the brightest bulb on the tree. A touch of lipstick seemed in order.

Millie offered up her hearts-and-horses plastic bracelet, so long as she got it back. Anne gave a solemn promise and put it on her wrist. The babysitter arrived on time and everyone agreed she was good to go.

Dom opened the door as she walked up the drive. He stood in a pool of light looking good in jeans and a jersey.

So much for listening to Sam, Anne thought. As she got nearer he didn't attempt to hide the fact he was ogling her.

'Wow,' he said, looking her up and down. Then he looked past her and said, 'you'll have to excuse me but I'm waiting for someone called Anne. Perhaps we can do this another time?'
'Funny guy,' she said, thrusting a bottle of supermarket red in his direction. 'Don't ask me what it tastes like.'

He stood back and gestured for her to come in. In her heels, she was almost as tall as him. He caught the smell of shampoo and perfume as she moved purposefully into the lounge.
'Nice,' Anne said. 'It's been a long time since I stepped foot in here. You've done a good job.' She turned to see him staring at her and commented on it.
He apologised and looked away.
'I didn't say I minded,' Anne said. She surprised herself with that comment and quickly began to worry he'd think she was coming on to him. He appeared not to have noticed and was making his way to the kitchen.

'Make yourself comfortable,' he said. 'I know you don't have very long so I thought I'd forgo a big meal and do nibbles instead.'
Anne felt her stomach twitch. She'd been working all day and had skipped lunch in the expectation of a blow out. 'Perfect,' she answered.

She sat on the sofa and then thought better of it. If he sat next to her, she wasn't ready for what might follow. By the time he returned with a tray of goodies she'd made a good attempt at looking relaxed in an armchair.

Dom sat a comfortable distance away. He looked tired, she thought. They leaned towards one another, chinked glasses and sipped the wine. He'd done well. The lighting was pleasant and no mood candles were evident. He'd acknowledged the fact that she wasn't staying and, so far, he'd been complimentary but not overly so. He knew how to make her feel comfortable. She began to relax.

'So,' Dom said, 'I think I should begin by apologising for my behaviour at the pub.' It was an insincere statement, but one he felt she probably expected. 'It's just that you caught me on the hop.'
Anne accepted the apology in good grace. 'I kicked myself for days afterwards,' she confessed. 'When I get it wrong it's usually with both feet.'
Dom waived it aside and said, 'let's start again. Tell me about you and Alice.'

It seemed a reasonable question and touched on common ground. Alice was someone they could both relate to. So, Anne gave a brief summary of her childhood memories involving Alice. Dom seemed intrigued, she noticed. He edged forward on his seat and hung, unblinkingly, on every word. When she finished, he'd backtrack on what she'd said and tried to tease out more and more information. Only when it became obvious that she was finding his persistence uncomfortable, did he back off.

He stood up to fetch the wine bottle and changed subject. 'So why cows?'
'We understand one another,' Anne said.
'Can't be easy running the place yourself?' He sat down and refreshed her glass.
'Terry helps,' she said, 'he's the young chap I saw you talking to at Millie's party.'
Dom passed a plate of snacks in her direction. 'What will you do when he leaves next month?'
The snack didn't make it to Anne's mouth. She locked eyes on Dom.
'What do mean, next month?'

Dom pinched his lips together and looked skywards. He sighed. 'You know that thing you said about going in with both feet?' He put his plate down and began rubbing his knees anxiously. 'I'm sorry. I just assumed you knew. That's what we were talking about. He signed up to some agriculture course.'

Anne drummed her lips with her fingertips and stared into the middle distance. 'Bugger,' she groaned.

Dom was annoyed with himself. The evening was only just underway and he'd put a spanner in the works. There was so much more he wanted to learn about Alice. It was irritating, but he could hardly shift the topic back until they'd dealt with this. He had to follow it through. With no great enthusiasm he asked what Terry did on the farm.

Anne struggled to re-engage. 'All sorts,' she said. 'He helps with the calves, the milking, machinery maintenance, all the stuff that makes a farm tick.' It was hard to be polite. 'Why didn't Terry say something?' she said, thinking aloud.
'Can't you hire someone else?' Dom asked.
'Around here?' The retort came out more sharply than intended. She pulled herself up and tried to explain. 'I was lucky to get Terry. Kids just move on. They aren't interested in farm work. It's a messy, smelly, hard job, that pays badly.' She checked her watch. She'd been there less than an hour but she needed to get her head around this and make decisions. She stood up, noticing an alarmed expression on Dom's face. 'I'm really sorry, Dominic but I have to go. Please don't take it personally.'

Dom found himself in a position where he could hardly say no. He stood up and on a whim said, 'I can help you out, if you'd like?'
She raised her eyebrows incredulously. 'That's lovely,' she managed to say, 'but I'm sure you have enough on your plate with writing.' She moved towards the door. 'Maybe when things are settled we can try again.'
'I'd like that very much,' Dom said. He watched as she hurried away,

wishing he'd kept his mouth shut. He closed the door, picked up his glass and chugged the contents. Walking over to Alice's photograph he picked it up and looked at her through sad eyes. You never told me you were in the school swimming team, he thought.

Then he sensed a change in the room. He turned around and there was the girl.
She stood on the opposite side of the room with her hands crossed in front of her.
Dom had a belly full of red wine and he felt emboldened.
'If it isn't my resident hallucination.' He slumped onto the sofa and reached for the bottle. 'Tell me, does being a ghost give you a free pass to listen in on other people's private conversations?'
She looked back, stone faced.
Dom got a fit of the giggles. He'd had a couple of large glasses before Anne arrived. His laughter stopped as quickly as it started. 'I wonder if you know what you are? Do you?'
She tipped her head to one side and studied him quizzically.
Dom could feel his head swimming, but he was still in charge of his faculties to ask more questions. 'Why don't you come when I call? Look at me, I'm knackered from sleepless nights thinking you might turn up in the shower, or watch me while I'm having a dump. And you never speak. Can't spooks, speak?'

Spooks speak, he repeated to himself. He looked at the bottle and chuckled. When he looked back, she had gone.

***

After a fitful night's sleep Dom found an excuse to contact ghost hunter Harry Wells. After a brief exchange of pleasantries, he got to the point. 'I wanted to ask you about your visits here,' Dom said. 'Why this house in particular?' He could almost hear Harry Wells scratching his head on the other end of the phone.

'Old properties tend to have the more interesting histories,' Harry said vaguely.

Dom said: 'but what about those interesting readings on your first visit.'

Harry sensed an opportunity. 'Why, have you been experiencing unexplained phenomena yourself, Mr Ross?'

'You first,' Dom said.

Harry was an enthusiast but he was no liar. He said that 99 per cent of their findings were easily explained. It was the one per cent that interested him and his colleagues. On their first visit they thought they'd picked up audio traces and temperature variations. Then, after a pause, he said the findings could also be explained by feedback within the equipment itself, or anomalies they were simply unable to explain, but which could have an explanation.

Dom was disappointed, but not surprised. Part of him hoped that Harry might reveal a story of the phantom girl who stalked the grounds. It wasn't to be.

'Of course it was the Wilson's who invited us in the first place,' Harry continued. 'They reported objects being moved around, lost, or being found in strange places. Not that we managed to record anything. Can I ask why you're interested, Mr Ross?'

Dom had his answer prepared. He said he was concerned at the fact that his property was splashed over the website as a haunted house. Two things bothered him, one of which was the fact he didn't want people poking around while he was trying to work and secondly the potential effect on the property price. When it came time to sell, he didn't want buyers put off by the inference that the place was haunted.

Harry confessed that he'd never even thought of that. Nobody had ever complained before, and he even wondered if a haunted house was a selling point. He sensed he was getting nowhere and supposed if Mr Ross was that concerned he could ask Tom to take it off the website. Dom said he appreciated the help and hung up.

A thought crossed his mind. Previously he'd wondered if the girl he'd been seeing was mentally ill. But, who would come over as the crazy one? He tried to imagine talking to someone about his experiences. Any sensible person would think he needed help. If he actually sought that help, what would they think? He imagined the conversation:

So, tell me what's been troubling you?
My house is haunted.
Why would you say that?
Because she appears to me.
The ghost is a woman?
I've just said that.
Does this ghost say or do anything?
No, she just stands and looks at me. Oh, and she can play the piano.
Didn't you say your wife played the piano?
I can see what you're thinking, but it's not like that. She looks like someone from the past.
The past?
I don't know, Victorian or Edwardian maybe.
Aren't you a writer of historical novels?
You keep trying to form associations.
It's because the ghost you refer to is most likely a metaphor. She's a way of representing your conflicted emotions and guilt over the loss of your wife. You said it yourself; you bought the house she was brought up in as a child. That's quite unusual. It suggests a form of attachment that is quite severe. Unresolved grief can be both powerful and disturbing. Perhaps we should talk about treatment?

Perhaps it was best kept to himself he thought.

6 THE PROTEST

Sam regretted not checking the weather forecast before chaining herself to the library doors. Summer had taken the day off, to be replaced by cold gusty winds and drizzle. On the plus side, the guy from the local press said it would generate sympathy for her cause. He took a few snaps, pulled up his anorak collar and asked directions to the pub.

A few minutes later Anne appeared with a flask and sandwiches. 'Sam the suffragette, I presume?' She dipped down next to her friend. 'Cheese or ham?'
'Bit early,' Sam said. 'I've yet to acquire drawn cheeks and a haunted look.'
'Unlikely, in the space of two hours,' Anne scoffed.
Sam eyed the sandwiches and said, 'cheese then.' She filled her mouth and began talking. 'You know,' she chomped, 'I don't think this place deserves a library. All these signatures yet not one person has turned out to join the protest. Community action shudders to a halt due to weather. Still, I should at least get a column in the local press.'

A pulse of cold wind caused them both to screw up their faces. 'You should quit now,' Anne said. 'Look, if the man from the press has been you've made your point. Anyway, you'll get piles from sitting on that wet floor.'
Sam looked unconvinced. 'I thought that was a myth?' She tried to stand and quickly realised the chains prevented it. 'Right then, protest over. Help me find the keys.' They fumbled in her pockets until it became clear the keys weren't to be found. Sam adopted a faraway look and remembered putting them on the counter.

The library doors were not locked, but Sam had wrapped the chain around the handles and herself. When Anne looked through the

39

window she saw them immediately.

'You utter chump,' she scoffed. 'The only way these chains are coming off is with a hacksaw.'

Sam let rip with a stream of exotic profanity. When she calmed down, she asked Anne whether she had cutting equipment on the farm. Anne said yes, but the round journey would take an hour. With little other option, Sam agreed.

Time passed. Sandwiches had been eaten and the rain came down in rods. Sam curled up in a ball of misery. A puddle had formed in the doorway and her attempts at keeping her shoes dry had long failed.

She heard a car pull up. Instead of Anne, she was confronted by Dom's startled expression. 'It's a protest against the library closure,' she called out. She rattled her chains and was about to make a crack about bondage when self-pity overwhelmed her. She lowered her head and began to sob.

Moments later she felt something being draped over her shoulders. She looked up. Her hair was stuck to her face. Her eyes were red and her nose was running. She liked that he looked genuinely concerned for her. 'I really think you should call it a day,' Dom said.

Sam sniffed and leaned into her sleeve to wipe her nose. 'I hadn't thought of that,' she said sarcastically.

He looked bewildered, so she told him the sorry saga, at which point he burst out laughing. She started to cry again.

He apologised, put his arm around her shoulders and gave a gentle squeeze, which she liked.

She sensed he was trying to think of ways out of her predicament and told him help was on its way.

He sat with her in the rain and poured coffee from the flask Anne had left.

Sam was unable to reach down, so he held the cup to her lips. She was in mid sip when a flash went off. They turned to see the reporter leaning out of his car with his camera. He gave a thumbs-up and drove off.

'I guess that's one for social media,' Dom said. He used his fingertip to move a strand of wet hair from Sam's eye and returned her grateful smile with a wink.

'Local rag,' Sam said. She was perking up and felt in the mood for a bit of banter. 'He was here earlier. He's writing an in-depth analysis about the demise of library facilities being a symptom of impending social collapse.'

Dom was impressed. 'Really? That sounds more like *Guardian* territory.' Sam rolled her eyes. Add dumb to odd, she thought. He was supposed to be a writer. Did he honestly think the local press was interested in much beyond the biggest marrow competition? But when she looked at him she softened.

He was fussing with the blanket around her shoulders and was acting as a windbreak to protect her from the elements. He had a kind of puppyish charm and sensitivity that touched her. 'Yes it does,' she agreed.

Anne turned up with some hefty bolt-cutters. She and Dom exchanged an awkward glance before he offered to use them.

Anne looked him up and down. She figured she had the advantage on muscles and set to it. A couple of well placed snips and Sam was free. Dom helped her to her feet and gathered up the chains.

They went inside and Sam bolted the door. 'Afternoon closure,' Sam said, then she took herself to the locker room.

Anne followed. She pointed to the kitchen area and asked Dom to make them all hot drink.

Sam stood in front of the full-length mirror feeling as wretched as she looked. Anne tugged at her soaking jacket, trying to peel it away. She reminded Sam of those wartime recruitment posters for land girls. Anne was tall, slim, rosy-cheeked and vital. Sam was none of these things. She was a smidge over five feet tall and teetered constantly on the edge of being overweight. On bad days, she thought her hair was too fine, her complexion needed sand blasting, and her boobs were too big; not that she'd received any complaints in that department.

Anne passed her an old curtain and said it would do for a towel.

'So,' Sam said, patting herself down, 'how did it go with Mr nice guy? Did you let him cop a feel?' She felt something soft hit the back of her neck.

Anne's voice lifted an octave, 'how ever did you become a librarian? No jobs left at the fish-market, were there?'

'The sound of the frustrated fertile woman,' Sam said. 'Not pretty.' She pulled on an oversized jersey someone had left and began adjusting the sleeve length.

'He's probably miffed,' Anne said. 'He said Terry was quitting next month and it threw me out. I left early.'

Sam turned to face her friend. 'Are you serious? You actually walked out because spotty Terry is leaving?'

Anne looked uncomfortable. 'Well, when you say it like that it, it sounds bad. It just threw me out. He's fifty per cent of the labour force. I had to get my head around it.'

Sam dug her hands into her hips, stepped forward and invaded Anne's personal space. She looked up, eyes glaring. 'The only place your head is, is up your backside. You should pull it out and get a life.' She pointed to the door. 'That man is as hot as they come and he probably fancies you. Chances like that don't turn up every day. If you don't see this as an opportunity, someone else will, and soon.'

Anne stepped back. 'Alright tiger, steady on.' Her brow puckered. 'I get it what you're saying. But all he was really interested in was talking about his dead wife. It was hardly the prelude to a romantic evening.'

There was a tap on the door. Dom announced that drinks were being served in the library.

They sat around a table and sipped tea.

Dom watched the way Anne held her cup, just below her lower lip, the way Alice did. She caught his eye and he quickly thought of something. 'Have you spoken to Terry yet?'

Anne shook her head. 'It's his day off.'

Dom ran a finger around the rim of his cup. 'You know, I meant it when I said I'd help out. I'm actually pretty good with my hands.'

Sam's mouth formed an "O". She winked at Anne, who feigned not to notice.

Anne was diplomatic. She smiled and said it was certainly something she would bear in mind if she was unable to replace, Terry.

As Dom focused his attention on Anne, so Sam studied Dom.

Dom finished his drink and said he needed to push on.

Sam thanked him for feeding her coffee.

Anne cast a hand in a goodbye gesture.

The friends spent some moments lost in their respective thoughts. Anne was the first to break the spell. 'He looked tired, don't you think?'

Sam agreed. Since looking carefully at Dom she had formed another opinion, 'and he's in pain.'

'Why do you say that?' Anne asked.

'The way he looked at you sometimes. There's stuff going on beneath the surface. I'm telling you, that is one sad man.'

Anne looked interested. 'You think so? I hadn't picked up on that.'

Sam pulled a face. 'Well, you surprise me.'

***

Dom unpacked his suitcase. He hadn't expected much of the room at *The Bomber*, but it was actually clean and cosy. At least tonight he hoped he would get a decent sleep and not have to worry about spooks and spectres.

He sat on the bed, unzipped a pocket and took out a leaflet. On the front was a glossy picture of a young woman with flip-floppy blonde hair and an earnest expression. She looked more like a beautician, he thought, but beneath it said, Dr Kirsten L. Moore, psychiatrist. He flicked it open to see a bullet-point list of services offered.

At £350 an hour, the fees were eye watering. With the extras, fifty quid per prescription, and the same again per referral, he wondered how anyone could afford it. He conjured an image of her Porsche and second home in Miami. Then he remembered the flow of conversation he'd had with himself earlier and tore it in two. If he really was tipping over the edge they'd just have to section him.

He stretched out on the bed and tried to think. If all this was in his head, he reasoned, it would reveal itself whether or not he was in the house. If not, what was his next course of action? He quickly dismissed the idea of involving Tom, Dick and Harry. They were no more than hobbyists and would probably fill their respective trousers if this Alice Drew revealed herself to them.

It upset him thinking about Alice Drew. Perhaps it was the association with his wife's name and the whole issue of death that was the problem. Well, apparently Alice Drew was a teacher therefore he would think of her simply as, Miss Drew.
It helped him to refocus. What was she doing in the house? What did she want, or need? Did she even know she was a ghost, but then maybe ghosts don't? His head throbbed from lack of sleep.

When Dom next checked his watch he realised he'd been asleep for ten hours. He felt like a man reborn.

7 ALICE DREW AND APPLE PIE

Unsmiling and in a rush, the woman who emerged from Dominic's house barely gave Sam a second glance as she brushed past. Sam watched as she slammed her car door shut and began making phone calls. Bad timing, Sam thought. She was about to walk away when she heard Dom's voice.

'Sam? What brings you here?'

Sam walked to the door and presented him with a neatly folded blanket.

'Just returning your Good Samaritan blanket. Plus, I have a gift.'

Dom ushered her inside, glancing briefly at his departing guest.

Sam took in her surroundings. There were easy chairs with silk cushions, a limed-oak coffee table and expensive rugs. On one wall, an art nouveau mirror, on another a group of small oil paintings. A spray of flowers from the garden lay on a sideboard waiting to be arranged. It was tasteful, relaxing, and - feminine. Dom was standing by the door, looking through a little glass panel.

Sam asked: 'Is that your mum?'

'God, no. She's only five years older than me. That's what happens to a literary agent with me onto their books.'

'I take it she's not happy?'

Dom stepped forward to relieve her of the blanket. 'Something like that.' He looked hesitant.

Sam took charge and told him to put the kettle on.

'What's this about a gift?' He called from the kitchen.

Sam told him he'd get his present, if her coffee came with biscuits or cake. A few moments later a tray with coffee and biscuits arrived. They sat next to one another on the big soft sofa. Sam grabbed a biscuit and began to graze. 'Now,' she said, spitting crumbs, 'I've got this for you.' She reached inside her coat and produced a few pages of A4, stapled at the corner.

Dom smiled at her easy company and plucked the pages from her fingers. 'And this is, what exactly?'

'A potted history of your new home.'

'Much obliged,' Dom said, and set the sheets down on the coffee table. Sam stopped munching and looked peeved. She picked the sheets back up and placed them on Dom's lap. 'There's work gone into this, Dominic. I want you to read it and be impressed by my many hours of labour.'

Dom laughed nervously. 'I shall place it on the very top of my to-do pile.'

Sam let it go and looked around the room again. 'Bet you didn't know it's meant to be haunted.' He turned and looked at her intently. 'Ah, that got your attention,' she said.

Dom made a conscious effort to relax his shoulders. 'Actually, I did. Some guys from a psychic society door-stepped me when I first got here.'

'Oh, Harry Wells and Co. What did they tell you?'

'Something vague about interesting readings.'

Sam helped herself to another biscuit. She studied it briefly. 'You should get the jammy one's' she said, 'much nicer.'

'I'll try to remember,' said Dom.

'Someone did die here though,' she said, getting back on track, 'all very sad.'

Dom went pale. He shakily put his cup down and loudly drew in a breath.

'You alright?' Sam asked guardedly. She remembered that pained expression. Talk of death and ghosts might be just a tad insensitive, she thought. Why hadn't she just turned around at the door? She took a quick gulp of coffee and looked at her watch. 'Is that the time?' She made to stand up, then felt Dom's hand on her forearm.
'I'm fine,' he smiled, 'reaction to boring biscuits maybe.' He held up the plate for Sam to take another. 'Help me shift these and I'll resupply,' he said.
She giggled with relief and helped herself to another.
'Press on,' Dom said, 'I'm all ears.'

Sam told him that when the place was a school a fire broke out. 'The young teacher, who was called Alice Drew, thought she'd got all the kids out, but when she did a head count, she thought there was one missing. She panicked, ran back inside and, well, didn't come out.'
'Alice,' Dom repeated to himself. 'And the boy?'
'That's the tragedy. She'd simply miscounted. Easily done, I suppose, in all the confusion.' Her voice trailed off as she watched Dom put his head in his hands. 'You're not fine, are you? There's something wrong?'

Dom emerged from behind his hands and avoided eye contact. He hunched forward and stared through the coffee table. 'Just the world catching up with me I think.'
Sam wrongly assumed this was some reference to the woman she'd just seen. 'Writer's block?' she enquired.
She had unwittingly thrown Dom a lifeline. One he was happy enough to grab.
'Block, gridlock, barrier, obstruction; all of things and more,' he complained.
Sam nodded sympathetically, wondering what to do or say next.

Dom returned to the topic of Alice Drew. 'Quite a few people lived here. Don't you find it odd how only some said they felt a presence? I don't remember my Alice saying anything about ghosts.'

47

'I read a book about that,' Sam said. 'In fact, in my line of work I read a great many books between customers.' She leaned in towards Dom, resting on her elbow. 'I've even read some of yours.' She gave him a knowing eyebrow flash. 'Credit where it's due, Dominic, you know your Tudors.'

Dom brushed aside the compliment. He wanted Sam to focus. 'What did it say? In your spook book.'

Sam squeezed one eye shut. It was something she did when trying to remember things. She said a common theme was unfinished business. The spirit remains behind because of some troubling event, or something needing to be done. The dilemma for the spirit was twofold. First, they didn't realise they were actually dead, and second they didn't know what they were meant to resolve. Basically, they were in limbo.

'So, how do they get passed that?' Dom asked.

Sam sat back up and checked her watch in earnest. 'You've exhausted my entire insight into the matter I'm afraid.' She stood up. 'Lunch break over; thanks for the coffee.'

'Well, what was the name of the book?' Dom persisted.

'I'll try and look it out.'

It was a short walk back to the library and Sam found herself thinking about Dom in ways her mother would describe as inappropriate. It wasn't just about his looks, it was the fact he was available, and so was she. There were only two constants in Sam's life. The first was her enduring friendship with Anne, who she would do anything for. It would such a good thing to see Anne hook up with Dom. If it worked out, and why wouldn't it, she'd have a partner and Millie would have a dad. The second was the library, and this was being taken from her. She might be able to get another job in a bigger library, but it would be a commute and a loss; this was her library, these were her books. She felt like Canute, trying to hold back the tide.

As she turned the corner she almost collided with Anne. Grinning from ear to ear, Anne slapped the local newspaper into Sam's hand. Sam opened the broadsheet and her jaw dropped. Not only had they run the story, it was all over the front page. The headline said, *Chivalry Lives On*. Beneath, was a picture of Dom kneeling in the soaking doorway. He was holding a cup up to Sam, who looked back at him adoringly. 'Oh, my God,' Sam squealed, 'I look like I've been run through a mangle. Look at the state of me. And what's this?' She began running indignant eyes down the article.

Anne stood next to her, trying to spot the problem. 'What's up?' 'They've made it all about him, that's what's up. Look,' she angled the paper in Anne's direction and began reading out the offending passage: *Popular author of historic fiction, Dominic Ross, takes pity on damsel in distress Samantha Wilson, during her self-imposed protest against library closure. Ross is best known for his trilogy, The Tudor Family. His fans patiently await his . .'* Sam gave up and crumpled the paper. 'Damsel,' she repeated through gritted teeth, 'self-imposed, indeed. I can forgive the picture, but where's the stuff about the library?'

Anne tried to be helpful. 'Surely what's important is the connection. People will read this and it will generate interest. You've got a celeb on your side.'
Sam looked unconvinced. 'Maybe,' she conceded. 'Anyway, how did they know he was Dominic Ross?'
'I expect one of the editorial team recognised his face from a book.'

It was time to re-open for the afternoon, but there seemed little point. Since her regulars got wind of the closure they had started to make other arrangements, but the rot had set in earlier. Things that used to draw younger people in, namely free Internet, was no longer appealing. Everyone had a personal computer at home and everyone had broadband. Many newspapers were now free online. People were no longer limited by what was in stock. They could sit in the comfort of their home, pick any book they wanted and download it as an eBook. The local school did its bit by bringing the kids every so often, but even the school was under threat of closure. It made Sam miserable.

They sat around the reading table drinking coffee. Sam was comfort eating yet more biscuits. It didn't help that Anne looked so cheery. 'Shouldn't you be making yogurt, or something?' she said, sounding morose.

'I've left Terry in charge,' Anne said. 'And guess what, Dominic Ross was wrong about him. Terry was only thinking about leaving. He didn't say anything to me because he hadn't decided.'

Sam raised her mug. 'A toast to Terry.' Then, out of the blue, she remembered the photograph in the newspaper. The way she had been looking at Dom made her realise something deeper was happening inside. She pushed the thought to one side. 'So, does this mean you'll be finding some time for dishy Dominic?'

Anne looked thoughtful. 'It's been a while since I bought a new dress. I wonder if he likes homemade apple pie.'

Sam felt a twinge of envy. Oh, I'm sure he will, she thought – then winked to her friend.

8 CHANGES IN THE AIR

His ears still burning from the dressing down delivered by his agent, Dom was on a long walk, trying to get his career back on track. He had always used walking as a prelude to writing. It helped clear his mind and stimulate his thinking, but today it wasn't happening. He felt under pressure. His agent had run out of excuses for the delay of his fourth book. The contract she had painstakingly negotiated with a major television network to screen the entire series, was in jeopardy. Everything hinged on pulling the last book together.

It was just after Alice died that his third book hit the shelves. People loved what they read and they sympathised with his plight. The deadline for book four was extended, but he was learning that compassion evaporates quickly where business is concerned. To buy time he had lied to his agent about his progress, but with nothing to show, she had quickly seen through it.

He had notes, masses of them, scribbled in books and pinned to boards, still stored in boxes. But, his prevarication had reached its limits, for now there was an absolute deadline of three months. If the book wasn't on his agent's desk by then, he could start looking for a job in a call centre.

When he returned home a parcel was waiting for him on the doorstep.

He knew it was a book simply by its feel. When he tore the paper to reveal the contents his interest was piqued. It was the book Sam had promised to look out for him.

He kicked off his shoes, locked the door and settled into his favourite reading chair. He scanned the contents and found that much of the material was taken up by historical accounts of paranormal activity and some experiments, many Russian, aimed at eliciting or recording unusual events.

He was losing heart when he spotted a section on conjuring spirits. It was five direct quotations by people claiming to have summoned the spirits of the dead. It did not look promising. He was about to shut the book when he spotted some scribbled pencil notes. The writing was tiny, but he made out, *commonalities: unresolved grief, focused on a loved one, within the sphere of active psychic phenomena*. He unpacked the sentence in his mind. He wasn't sure if his grief was normal or unresolved, but it was certainly grief. Alice, of course, was his loved one. As for the so-called sphere of psychic phenomena, it could only be this house.

That tied the parts together but it left questions unanswered. Why were Miss Drew's appearances so haphazard? When he wanted to see her, when he called for her to appear, she stubbornly refused. She only seemed to show up when he least expected it. There had to be a link, but what was it? Dom struggled with ideas until he became too tired to continue.

His concerns began to edge back in the direction of work and his finances, when out of the blue it struck him. The last time Miss Drew appeared was when he was thinking about Alice. No, it was more than that, he was immersed in thinking about and talking to her. Could it really be that simple?

It was early afternoon and sun poured through the windows. He reached across for the photograph of Alice and began talking to it. He described the walk he'd just had along winding tracks bound by banks of cowslip. He waxed lyrical about clouds and birdsong, and he quickly realised it wasn't going to work.

Simply looking at Alice and talking to her photograph was a contrivance. The element missing, he realised, was pain, and that was something he couldn't simply conjure up. Not a day had passed that Alice hadn't occupied his thoughts, sometimes for hours. Yet, right now, when he needed the dark familiarity of that emotion, it eluded him. He grimaced at the irony and replaced the photograph.

**

Anne's approach to fashion was simple. Go online and find a tall, slim model, with red hair and see what she was wearing. If it looked alright she might try it herself.

The last time she'd paid out for a dress she was still with Kenny. They had been together since school and it had never really occurred to her things might change. Then she had what people describe as - one of those years. It began when her acrimonious parents split up, leaving her and dad to run the farm. She was forced to help out more, which meant less time messing around with Kenny. When they were together, they argued more.

Kenny sulked at the fact she appeared to choose the farm over him. One night, during yet another row, he asked if she still loved him. When she said yes, he kept challenging her to prove it. She gave in.

Sex was a hurried affair of grunting, pressing and groping on the back seat of Kenny's car. They did it twice that night. It wasn't exactly unpleasant, but with neither of them using protection, she couldn't relax. For Anne, it was more of a statement; a declaration that she was serious about their relationship. And she had proved it, just the way he'd asked.

Anne's dad had started to feel unwell and he reluctantly asked her to cover some of his jobs. As a result, she didn't see Kenny for a while. She began to worry when she missed her period. After another day of backbreaking work, she lumbered into the kitchen, hoping dad had cooked up a decent supper. She found him collapsed in a heap. His heart had given out. Anne's mum rushed back. She was guilt-laden and angry with everything. In the turmoil that followed, Anne's head was in the clouds.

After the funeral, Anne discovered the farm had been left to her. Mum wanted her to sell up, saying it had no future and it would destroy her. Anne saw this more as a reflection of her mother's unhappiness. What Anne wanted was some stability in her life. When she told Kenny about the pregnancy he seemed supportive. A week later, he'd gone. She never found out where, and she never made the effort to track him down. She felt betrayed and it broke her heart, but it also made her more determined to make a go of things.

Not for one minute did she think of terminating the pregnancy. Somehow, the baby seemed bigger than both of them and she couldn't imagine a better place to raise a child. Much to her surprise, her mother had been supportive of Anne keeping the child. She had never liked Kenny. In her eyes he was a lost cause from the outset; a village boy who would never rise above a cleaner or shelf stacker. But, she had always wanted grandchildren. She got the best of both worlds: a grandchild and Kenny out of her daughter's life.

The picture in the magazine lay on the bed. Anne adopted the same pose as the model and checked herself out in the mirror. Not too shabby, she thought. The olive green dress matched her eyes and flattered her body shape in all the right places. Sam was right, she thought. She'd been hiding herself away for too long. She was older and wiser and, persuaded by Sam, had finally given herself permission to have some fun. This time, she would take the initiative and invite

Dominic for dinner. It would be a way of apologising for their last encounter.

***

Sam walked slowly past the display cases, running her fingertips along the spines of the books. It was just a matter of time until the containers arrived. Some of the books would be distributed to other libraries many more would be disposed of. She knew the arguments and financial practicalities of closure, but part of her wondered if things could be done differently. She'd also seen the spread-sheets. Building maintenance, staff costs, stock resources, and a range of direct and indirect costs. It added up of course, and in times of cutbacks, services like libraries were always vulnerable.

As for herself, she still needed an income. Sentimentality and demonstrations didn't pay bills. She wondered just how much her recent stunt had cost her in terms of goodwill with her employers. Nothing had yet been said and the silence was deafening.

Her phone buzzed. There was an image of Anne striking a pose in her new dress. She looked good, but then Anne would look good in a bin bag. The only thing holding Anne back from whatever she wanted was a lack of confidence. When they were together, the banter flowed freely. More often, she was less certain of herself and more risk averse, yet in other ways she had resilience. She had doggedly held onto the farm and made it work. She would do anything for her daughter, Millie, and as a friend, she was totally honest and reliable.
Sam texted back: *Looks a bit fancy for milking cows.*
She got a LOL in return.

Sam tried to be as good a friend in return, but she had a secret shame. It was that she'd had a brief dalliance with Kenny while he was still technically with Anne. It was during the time Anne retreated into working on the farm. Weeks had gone by and Anne became an out-of-sight, out-of-mind period in Sam's life.

Kenny was a decent enough looking guy and she was no saint. When Kenny turned to her, she was at a loose end and she liked the attention. One night they both drank too much which ended in a quickie at the back of the pub. Only their combined guilt prevented the news getting out. If it had, her friendship with Anne would be shattered. They were all younger then, but it was a poor excuse. The thought she might lose her friend now was unbearable.

9 ANNIVERSARY

Miss Drew next appeared when Dom was at a low point and he could easily have done without it. Today would have been his wedding anniversary and every cell in his body felt like lead. He was immersed in memories and speculation about a life that might have been. His pain and anguish was the calling card for Miss Drew.

Dom, the man of reasoning, had always dismissed the notion of an afterlife. Both he and Alice believed that once people checked out, that was it, game over. If anything, Alice was the harder-nosed. She resented people coming to the door on recruitment drives for their faith. Whereas Dom would say a polite no thanks, she would take them on and have a full-blown argument. Yet, in her last few days, even she had begun to wonder if there was more.

Dom rarely left her bedside, but on one occasion, as he stepped out of the lift, he saw a vicar leave her room. He never asked why, but he did notice she seemed more at peace. At the time he put it down to fear and vulnerability, but it didn't matter to him. If Alice had wanted them to sign up as Scientologist's, he would have said pass the pen: anything to put her mind at ease.

Miss Drew adopted her favoured position of looking out of the window into the garden. This time, Dom tried to step back from his pain and to free his mind from the constraints of rationality. Miss Drew was here, in front of him, and he would work with that. They had something in common; they were both lost souls.

She was from a time where manners and the roles of men and women were very different. If he could meet her halfway, there was just a chance he might learn a few things. It was no easy thing, fighting against his mood, but he made the effort. He stood upright, with his hands behind his back. 'How good of you to call, Miss Drew,' he said hesitantly.

She turned and smiled in acknowledgement.

Dom felt his pulse quicken. She could hear and respond.

He pressed on. 'Would you care to sit?'

She sat on the arm of a chair, her back ramrod straight, hands folded on her lap. Dom stood still, worried that any movement might disrupt the moment. 'I wondered,' he continued, 'might I ask you about your memories of Miss Alice Ross,' he corrected himself, 'I mean Peters, Alice Peters.'

Miss Drew smiled as though she could recall the memory. She stood up, and for a moment Dom thought she would leave, but she looked back out into the garden.

There was a tap at the door and Miss Drew had gone.

He stood still for a moment. It was the weirdest feeling. How could anyone hope to explain how it felt to communicate with a ghost? It was like first contact with an alien species. There were so many questions. The tapping on the door became more insistent.

Irritated by the intrusion, Dom flung open the door to see the open-mouthed gaze of a small man, dressed in safari jacket, and sporting a comb-over.

The man began to smile. 'It's you, isn't it?'

'Yes, it is most definitely me,' Dom answered, his voice clipped and dripping with sarcasm. 'Now we've established that, I'm closing the door.'

'Wait,' said the man urgently. He rummaged in his man-bag and pulled out a newspaper. 'Dominic Ross: I'm a big fan.' He pulled open the broadsheet to reveal the image of Sam chained to the library door and thrust it forward. 'I'm almost your neighbour,' he babbled, 'well, about a forty-minute drive off, but that's nothing is it?'

Dom scanned the paper and the realisation that his anonymity was over, began to hit home. Strictly speaking he had never actually sought isolation. In fact, living in a city was the next best thing to solitude he could think of. Nobody really looked at anyone because it was a sea of faces wherever you went. Then again, nobody really knew about Dominic Ross, until some media campaign started pushing the television series. He'd done the rounds of author talks and book signings, but these had dwindled to virtually nothing since Alice died. No wonder his agent was apoplectic. He was contractually obliged to finish the final book in the series and do the promotional rounds, yet here he was, still in self-imposed isolation.

The man had turned around and taken a step back. Dom realised he was taking a selfie. Oh well, he thought, if it goes viral or whatever these things do, his agent would be over the moon.
'Would you mind signing for me?' Without waiting for an answer he pulled out the first of the Tudor books. 'It's to Gordon, if you don't mind.'
In for a penny, thought Dom. The man passed him a biro and Dom wrote, *Happy reading, Gordon. Best wishes*. He scrawled his signature and did a quick doodle of a Tudor Rose. Gordon looked delighted.
As Dom returned the book, a thought came to mind. He adopted a conspiratorial tone. 'Listen Gordon, if you wouldn't mind keeping my address between us, I'd be most grateful. You know how it is with tourists rolling up by the bus load, can't get a thing done.'
'No worries,' Gordon said, tapping the side of his nose, 'mum's the proverbial.'
'You're a chum,' Dom said and quickly closed the door before Gordon could think of anything else to say or do.

He went upstairs and looked out of the window, half expecting to see a coach party wandering down the lane towards his house. Then he checked himself. Who exactly did he think he was? A single man knocking on his door meant nothing. In any case, authors aren't celebrities in that sense, he thought. In his experience, people tended to be terribly British. He assumed most avid readers were inclined towards introversion anyway, which probably explained it. Gordon, therefore, was something of an anomaly.

As he turned to go downstairs, something struck him. His mood had lifted. Since seeing Miss Drew and chatting to Gordon he felt different - lighter somehow. It felt good. He picked up the photograph of Alice and gave it a kiss. 'Happy anniversary, sweetheart,' he said. He put the photograph down and looked outside. It was a glorious day. Where were his shoes?

10 ASSET STRIPPING

Dom picked up the book Sam had lent him and headed off to return it to her. He felt like he'd woken from a dream-laden sleep and life's equilibrium was being slowly restored. He was invigorated and decided on the longer of two walks he'd previously mapped out. He ran his fingers through his hair and realised it was way past collar length. Maybe there was a place in the village where he could get it cut?

The track he took passed around farmland and finished at a small car park on the edge of the village. Just as he was crossing it, a mini-coach pulled in. At any other time, he would have thought nothing of it, but after Gordon's visit, he was more alert. He put his head down and picked up the pace.

Inside the library a couple of people were browsing the shelves. He could see Sam at the far end, with what looked like a laundry skip on wheels. She turned at the sound of the little bell on the door and lifted a finger to indicate she'd seen him.

Dom looked around. He'd been here before but hadn't really paid much attention to the surroundings. The place wasn't much bigger than a small supermarket, but Sam had an eye for organisation. She'd managed to squeeze a reading table in the children's section, and there were a couple of Internet terminals against the window. He noticed these had been disconnected. It dawned on him what Sam was doing. She was filling the container with books in preparation for the library closure.

He walked around, checking the titles on the spines. His mind drifted to something he'd once heard about never feeling alone in a bookshop. It was true. He loved libraries and what they represented. They pulled together the seemingly contradictory functions of refuge and community, sanctuary and activity. He paused to look back over the shelves. The reading preferences of the villagers seemed biased towards general fiction, romance and crime. There was also a good selection on cooking and gardening. He picked one that caught his eye about small garden design and thumbed the pages.

Sam joined him. 'Thinking of spreading seeds,' she said cheekily. The woman is incorrigible, Dom thought, but he couldn't help smiling. 'What a grubby mind you have,' he said. 'Thank goodness I didn't pick up something on vegetables.'
'There's so much more in here,' Sam replied, tapping her head. Dom's expression conveyed that he believed her. 'I've returned the book you left for me,' Dom said, 'it's on the counter.'
'There's a fee for overdue books,' Sam said. She leaned into him. 'In your case it's lunch at the pub.'
'Nice try,' he said. He rested his hands on her shoulders, intending to move her away, but as he did so he looked into her eyes. They conveyed such deep sadness that it stopped him in his tracks. 'Sam, what's the matter?'
Sam buried her forehead into his chest. He felt her body shudder as she let out a single anguished sob. He tried to look at her face, but it was too soon. The prospect of being separated made her cling to him.
He had a flashback to Alice when she was ill. He found himself drawing Sam in and stroking the back of her head.
The worst of the distress quickly subsided and Sam began to sniff. She released her grip and tried to make light of the situation by saying garden design books always had that effect on her. When she stepped

back she felt a handkerchief against her cheek. She reached up to take it and her hand touched the back of his.

Dom didn't move. It had been so long since anyone had been in his arms he had almost forgotten the sensation. He felt Sam's fingertips glide across the back of his hand. He sensed her face inclining towards his own and realized this was something he wanted.

A flash of light interrupted the moment. They both turned in its direction, rapidly releasing their hold like a pair of guilty teenagers. Two more flashes went off. A small crowd had gathered outside the library. One of the women looked at them with puppy eyes and appeared to making a sound like, aahh! Dom recognised her as one of the people he'd seen disembarking from the coach. Some of them were chained together with what looked like a string of silver foil hoops. There were placards: *Hands off the Library*, *Books Matter*, *Love Your Library*. Another pressed the front page of the local paper against the window. A girl wore a t-shirt with *Dom Ross Rocks*, emblazoned across the chest. Dom guessed there were about twenty of them, nearly all women.

'I think I've just shit myself,' Sam said.

Dom stood transfixed, trying to work out his next move. Some were holding up phones obviously filming. In a nanosecond this would be over social media.

'We're being filmed,' he mumbled, his mouth forming a stiff smile. He took Sam's hand and raised it in the air like she'd won a grand victory. The crowd cheered and clapped. 'You'll have to say something,' Dom said.

'What will I say?'

'What were you going to say last time, when nobody turned up?' He let go of her wrist then ran his hand to the small of her back and began pressing her forward.

'Don't push,' she hissed. By now she had also formed a rictus grin and began to wave back. 'And don't try to get out of it.'

Sam opened the door, briefly wondering why none of them had opened it themselves. 'Oh, my God,' she squealed, 'I don't know what to say.' That's a first, Dom thought.

The one wearing the t-shirt grabbed him: she extended her arm and angled her phone for a selfie. Twice in one day, Dom thought, I'm already sick of it. He smiled generously while they stood motionless for a second, then she let him go.

The gabbling settled down and one of them started to speak. 'We've come from Norwich to offer some support. Your chain protest is all over social media. Everyone is sharing and talking about it. What would you like us to do? Shall we chain ourselves to the door?'

Sam extended her arms and slowly shook her head. 'That would be great. Sure, go ahead.'

Sam and Dom stepped to one side while the group gathered in a tight bundle around the doorway and arranged their paper chains. One of the men, still standing, pulled a large container of water out of a shopping trolley. It had a spray attachment.

'Tell me they're not about to do what I'm thinking,' Sam said. She half hid behind Dom.

The man called out, 'ready girls' and began to saturate them with water. His companion filmed the dousing. The group held their placards aloft. With matted hair and clothing that stuck to them they began singing to baa-baa black sheep:

Take our library,
Take our books away,
Where shall we go to on library day?
Cut out the library
We all feel the pain
Cos closing down a li-bra-ry is plainly insane

'Shoot me,' Sam groaned, pushing her head into Dom's back.

They finished and turned expectantly to Sam and Dom. Sam emerged from behind Dom's back, jumping up and down excitedly, clapping and whooping.

Dom managed a big smile and nodded his head approvingly. It was all the group needed. They repeated the verse continually.

'Oh crap,' Sam muttered under her breath. She smiled broadly, lifted her hands and pretended to conduct.

One of the local farmers emerged from the shop. He stood next to Sam, listened for a moment and scratched his head. He looked at Dom and declared, 'thas a rummun,' then continued on his way.

Moments later, an estate car pulled up and out stumbled the body, face and hair of local television legend, Mary Perry. She had a mass of crow-black hair, Hollywood teeth and bright red lipstick. She had a quick word with the cameraman and stood with her back to the group. The singers found an extra burst of energy. If they had sung Jerusalem, it could not have been performed with greater passion.

Mary was doing a piece to camera so it wasn't possible to hear what she was saying.

Dom made an attempt at slipping away, but was stopped by Sam who clamped a vice-like grip on his arm.

The lens of the camera positioned itself over Mary's shoulder as she turned to face Sam. She thrust a microphone in front of Sam who stood rigidly to attention.

'Quite a turn out,' Mary trilled, 'Where do you see the protest leading?' Sam surprised herself by quickly rising to the occasion. 'A protest is quite simply an action that expresses disapproval. We view any library closure as short-term expediency. The financial gains will be minor when set against the long-term effects on this community.'

Mary nodded furiously. It was a technique aimed at encouraging interviewees to speak. Over the years it had developed into a nervous habit that bore little relation to the nature of what was being said. Mary pulled the microphone back, still nodding. 'And what do you imagine these long term effects to be?'

'Libraries provide reading materials and resources to all age groups, regardless of their social background or income,' Sam replied. Her face stiffened as she outlined the perceived injustice. 'People who don't use libraries think they are stuffy buildings filled with dusty books. Nothing could be further from the truth. This is a small village library,' she gestured to the building behind her, 'yet we provide kids clubs, computer terminals, reading groups for all ages, and presentations from famous authors.'

She gestured towards Dom, who stood stone-faced. 'Dominic Ross, as you may know, is an acclaimed author whose work is about to be televised as a major series.'

It was clear that Mary didn't know, but she was astute enough to keep the camera rolling and point the microphone in Dom's direction. Dom caught the beginnings of a smirk appear on Sam's face, but he was cornered. He cleared his throat and tried to look serious. 'That's right. I agree with everything Sam has just said.'

Mary was nodding and apparently not listening. It left an awkward pregnant pause which Dom felt obliged to fill. 'Libraries have been systematically neglected over the years,' he said. 'Asset stripping only really works if the assets have been properly maintained, but libraries like this are already on their knees. Once the family silver has been sold there's nothing left. People should be out here, brandishing their library cards as symbols of defiance.'

'Where is yours?' Mary asked.

'That's easy,' Dom said looking furtively at Sam, 'I've just moved here, which is why Sam was setting me up with a card when our new friends arrived.' He gestured to the group huddled dripping in the doorway. He heard one of them mutter, 'so that's what they call it around here.'

Mary took a step back and faced the camera. 'Well that's all we've got time for here. I'll hand you back to the studio, because I'm about to join the protest.' The cameraman slid a finger across his throat to indicate he'd stopped filming and Mary's shoulders slumped. She turned to Sam.

'That will make for great viewing, thanks. Now, where can I can grab a single malt?'

Sam pointed in the direction of the pub. 'Thought you were joining the protest.'

Mary raised a cynical eyebrow and headed back to the car.

'Nothing is ever what it seems,' Dom said.

'Profound,' grunted Sam. 'Fancy a pint?'

'What about this lot? You can't just leave them?

Sam copied Mary's expression and began to walk away.

Dom quickly caught up.

11 KENNY

There had only ever been a handful of shops in the village but to discover yet another charity shop had opened seemed too much. Anne studied the odd arrangement of goods in the window and decided there was nothing of interest. They must import stuff from other places, she thought. There was no way this village provided that much stock. She checked her watch and began a slow walk to the school in order to collect Millie.

One of the other parents turned the corner, child in tow. Anne realised either her watch was slow or the kids had been let out early.

They passed a few comments and Anne made her excuses. The school came into view. She immediately spotted Millie standing with another child. Both children were holding the hand of a young school helper. The helper was wearing a high visibility vest and seemed preoccupied with chatting to a man on the other side of the railings.

As Anne drew closer, Millie spotted her. She threw up an energetic wave. Anne never tired of moments like this. They lifted her spirits in a way nothing else came close to doing. She smiled, waved back and reached into her pocket to find a small chocolate bar. It was when she looked more closely at the man that she felt her stomach lurch. Her pace slowed a little as she confirmed her suspicions. It was Kenny. He'd put on weight, grown a goatee and his hair was different, but it was him.

She heard herself saying no, no, as she began to run towards the school.

It took a few moments to reach the school gate. The helper was a cocky young thing Anne had never warmed to. She came out with some remark about slowing down and heart attacks, but Anne's attention was still on the man who had disappeared around the corner.
'Who were you talking to?' Anne asked, still catching her breath.
The helper gave a, what's-it-to-you look, then decided to turn it to her advantage. 'Bees around a honeypot,' she smirked.
Or a fly around shit, Anne thought.

Anne grabbed Millie and walked hurriedly away from the school. Mille protested they were walking too fast and that Anne was squeezing her hand. Anne realized she was in a panic and stopped. She stooped down, gave Millie a hug and said she was sorry. Then she passed her the bar of chocolate. All was forgiven.
Millie wanted to visit the duck pond on the way home. She had named a few of them and wanted to see what they were doing. Anne's mind was spinning. She was pleased for the distraction and so they went.

Ducks gathered around Millie, hoping for some morsel of food. She jabbered away to them while Anne sat on a bench and tried to collect her thoughts.
When at first Kenny ran away she was distraught, but seeing him by the school made her feel physically sick. She couldn't imagine what he was thinking. Did he seriously think he could come back after nearly seven years and become Millie's father? Not once had he acknowledged Millie as his own. He had never paid a penny in maintenance, never sent a present, and probably didn't even know Millie's birthday. His family would probably have given him some basic information, like her name. They may even have taken pictures of her. Anne's mum was right all along. He was a loser, a chancer and a waste of space.

Anne needed to talk to someone. She would ask her friend Sam. Sam was bound to know what to do.

***

Sam was locking the library door when she heard a shout. She turned to see Anne heading in her direction and felt a pang of guilt. The previous day, when Dominic comforted her, she thought there was a moment between them. When they went to the pub afterwards, nothing was said, but her radar told her something had changed between them. Seeing Anne, she knew she mustn't upset their fledgling relationship.

'Where are you going?' Anne asked.

Sam thumbed towards the library. 'No more lending and the shelves are being stripped, plus my back aches.' She could see Anne was distressed.

'Can we go somewhere?' Anne asked.

'Let's go to my place. Millie can watch cartoons.'

It was a short walk to Sam's cottage. When her parents died it passed to Sam as their only child. It was small, but solidly built. Sam's only gripe was the lack of light through the tiny windows. Even on sunny days she had to use artificial lighting. She put on the television. Millie sat crossed legged in front of the screen, becoming instantly immersed in the adventures of a squirrel.

The friends went into the kitchen and Sam boiled a kettle. Sam said: 'so, what's the problem?' She took a couple of mugs down from a shelf and dropped tea bags in them.

'I've just seen Kenny,' Anne answered.

Sam was startled; the memory of her own liaison with Kenny flooded back. It was lucky that Anne was staring at the floor, lost in her own thoughts. Sam collected herself. 'Are you sure it was him?'

Anne nodded. 'He was by the school, chatting up that bimbo that works there.' She gasped. 'Millie was just inches from him.'

Sam poured water into the mugs. 'Do you think he knew Millie was his?'

'She's not his,' Anne said, raising her voice. She saw Sam look past her to check if Millie was reacting. Anne lowered her voice. 'She was never his,' she said, 'and if he thinks just showing up like this will change that he's got another think coming.'

'Of course,' Sam said soothingly. 'But what have you told Millie about him?'

'So far she's been satisfied with, not all children have a mummy or daddy. A couple of the kids in her class are in the same situation.'

Sam tried a different tack. 'Look, we can't assume that's why he's here, or even that he's come back. He's got family here.'

Anne grasped the possibility. 'That's right,' she said. 'It might explain why he legged it the moment he saw me.'

'There you are. That's not the behaviour of someone who wants to get back into your life.'

'It's not me I'm bothered about. That's why I wanted to talk to you. I want to know if he has any rights of access to Millie?'

Sam shrugged. 'I think you'd need legal advice. I've a feeling he may have some rights in the matter.' She watched as despair etched across Anne's face. 'But I remember you saying he's never contributed a thing. That must count for something.'

Anne buried her face in her hands.

'Look, you need to be proactive,' Sam said. 'I'll get you the number of someone who knows about these things. At least you'll know the legal position.'

Anne dragged her fingers down her face and clung on to the little breakfast bar. 'How much will that cost?'

'Nothing, I hope. Just leave it with me. Meanwhile, can you get away for a few days with Millie?'

'No. Millie has school and I've got the farm. Maybe I'll just look out dad's old shotgun,' she said, scowling. 'Now pass me that tea.'

Sam saw it as a signal to change topic. After a pause she said: 'So when's that fancy new dress going to see some action?'

Anne flashed her a glance and smiled ruefully. 'Who knows?'

'Who knows,' Sam said incredulously, 'Have you asked him out yet?'

Anne looked uncomfortable. She looked up at Sam and said: 'it's really not that important to me Sam and anyway I know about you and Dominic.'

Sam looked startled. Her voice became shrill. 'What about *me* and Dominic? There is no, *me* and Dominic!'

Anne said nothing. She pulled out her phone, found what she wanted and showed it to Sam.

Sam's frown was deep set as she concentrated on the video. She quickly realized it must have been uploaded by one of the library demo group. It showed her and Dom locked in an embrace. Then came the moment when Sam looked up and Dom appeared to be on the verge of kissing her. 'This isn't how it looks,' Sam said forcefully.

'It's alright, Sam, really it is,' Anne said nonchalantly. 'I've got no claim on him and if you and he, well - you know.'

'No, I don't know,' Sam said. 'He just happened to turn up when I was feeling pretty crap. Quite honestly it could have been anyone.'
Anne looked doubtful. 'I have to get on. Thanks for the tea. I'd be really grateful for that number.'

It was Sam's turn to look distressed. 'Don't go like this, Annie, please. I promise, nothing happened.'
Anne gave her friend a kiss on the cheek. 'It doesn't matter if it did. We're good, I promise.'
Millie protested at leaving behind the best cartoon she had ever seen. Then they were gone.
Sam stared at the door closing. She hung her head and felt perplexed.

12 BLACKMAIL

Dom was on a roll. His newfound energy and focus was like the gift that kept on giving. All the scraps of paper and notes that once seemed so disparate suddenly had a pattern. It was like doing the last few pieces of a jigsaw puzzle: suddenly the end was in sight and the pieces just slotted in.

It was the pain in his neck and shoulder that finally persuaded him to stop typing. As always, his last act was to touch the photograph of Alice, only now it didn't tear at his heart. He didn't understand why his change in mood had come about, but he was grateful for it. It was only now, with a sense of hindsight that he began to realise how all consuming his grief for Alice had become.

Outside it was breezy and warm. He grabbed a notepad and pen, walked into the garden and sat beneath a silver birch. Dark leaves foreshadowed the coming of autumn but dappled sunlight cast shimmering hypnotic patterns across the garden.

He would have liked to talk to Miss Drew but, it appeared, the required levels of pain and bitterness had left him. He wondered if she was nearby, sharing this day with him. He hoped so.

He still didn't understand why Miss Drew was here. Such things were outside of normal comprehension. Today, he wasn't even certain she existed outside of his mind. Not so long ago, his anguish was such that his mind could easily have been playing tricks on him. He wanted her to be real, well, as real as a spirit could be. It seemed that she had a sense of place, whereas he was merely passing through. Of one thing he was certain, no Tom, Dick or Harry would intrude, not so long as he had a say in the matter.

Dom rested his head against the tree, enjoying the sun's heat as it caressed his body. His awareness of Miss Drew had passed. Had sleep not begun to overtake him, he might possibly have seen her starting to approach him.

***

The doors to the library were flung open to allow the breeze through. Container loads of books, journals, magazines and papers of all description lined the walls.
Sam grabbed the pile of previously ignored mail and began sifting through. She had a long list of agencies, publishing houses, people and places still needing to be contacted. It was a job she'd put to one side for her final fortnight of employment.
She sifted though the envelopes and found two addressed to her personally. The first offered her the opportunity of redeployment as a librarian. It was part-time, less money and at least an hour away by car. By the time she'd paid for petrol there wouldn't be much left over.
She ripped open the second envelope to learn there was no space in the remaining libraries, archives or storage facilities for the books. The cost of leasing additional storage facilities was deemed too expensive for the range and quality of reading provision. The options were, find a way to donate them or they would be collected for disposal.

Sam felt miserable. No job, no books, no point. She had a small amount of money put by. It would give her time, perhaps a few weeks, to consider other options but she couldn't imagine what these might be. Marvellous, she thought resentfully.
Someone entering the library attracted her attention. She knew by the sound of sniffing that it was Kenny. He had always sniffed when he was nervous and the years hadn't changed a thing.
'Miss me?' He put a cigarette in his mouth and leaned against the reception desk.

Sam regarded him with suspicion. What did he think he looked like? He was dressed head to toe in blue denim. The bottoms of his jeans were turned up, revealing a pair of old doc Martin boots. He sported an Armstrong Custer goatee and had a short back and side's haircut. His gaunt face and sunken eyes had the look of a druggie.

'No smoking,' Sam said pointing to the sign.

He rolled his eyes and snatched the cigarette dangling from his lower lip. He looked around. 'What's happening here, then?'

'Guess.'

He sniffed. 'Nice welcome,' he muttered.

Sam took a couple of steps towards him. She stood wide-legged with her hands on her hips. 'What do you want, Kenny?' she asked tersely.

Kenny crossed his arms defensively. 'What's up with you?'

He never was the sharpest tool in the box, Sam remembered. His good looks once compensated for the lack of vocabulary, but those days had long gone. He was always like this, Sam remembered. Information needed to be squeezed out of him. He was the type of person who phoned you, but then had nothing to say. Sam could easily tell him to sling his hook, but she would be left wondering what he was up to. She remembered Anne's fear and decided to make life a little easier for him until she found out more. 'If you want a smoke, we can go out the back,' she said.

Kenny brightened up. 'Cool.' He bounced on his toes. 'Any chance of a cuppa? Got any biscuits?'

The big kid was just below the surface, but that same kid could be stubborn and petulant. 'I'll see what we've got,' Sam said. What on earth did she ever see in him? Maybe when you're the only ram in the field that's what happens.

They went to the tiny courtyard at the back of the building. Kenny sat down warily and lit up. He blew a thin line of smoke between his legs and threw a hesitant glance in Sam's direction.

Sam left him alone and put the kettle on. She watched him through the window. The modest veneer of confidence had given way to a leg twitching with agitation. She couldn't begin to think what he was up to. She made tea. The biscuit tin was almost full, but there was no way convulsing Kenny was laying a finger on her jammy dodgers. She guessed he took sugar, so she left it out.

Kenny took a sip of the hot tea and pulled a face. 'Any sugar?'
'Sorry.'
He stubbed out his cigarette, reached for another, and then thought better of it.
'What have you been up to these past years,' Sam asked.
He brushed non-existent dust off his sleeve and stared at a weed poking between slabs. 'This and that,' he said evasively.
'Wow, impressive.'

Kenny's reaction was disproportionate. He jumped up and jabbed a finger in Sam's direction. 'Shut your mouth, bitch,' he shouted, 'what have you done that's so special? Book reading is it?'
He's deliberately pumping himself up Sam thought. Even so, she couldn't resist a retort. 'Well, that's something we could never accuse you of.'
He seemed on the edge of hitting out, or flouncing off, but something stopped him. He sat back down and gave Sam a calculating look. 'You still mates with Anne?'
'What sort of question is that?'
'Thought so,' he said. 'So, what do think she'd say if she found out about us?' He sniffed then flicked a finger between himself and Sam.

It took a moment for Sam to connect. When she did, she was incredulous. Her voice became shrill. 'Is this . . . are you trying to blackmail me, Kenny?'
Kenny shrugged. 'Wouldn't cost much for me to keep my mouth shut,' he said.
Sam burst out laughing.
Kenny remained hard-faced.
It had the desired effect. Sam's laughter came to an abrupt halt, but she was in no mood for Kenny's low-life tactics. 'You utter loser,' she said bitterly, 'I wouldn't give you my toenail clippings if you begged me for them.'

A tense silence fell between them. Your move, Sam thought. But of course you can't think, can you Kenny? So you're left with carrying out your threat, because you're obstinate. She began to feel more in control. Even if Kenny did go to see Anne, she would be in no mood for his antics. And what was the most he could he achieve? At best it would be his word against hers, and surely Anne wouldn't listen to the creep? Even so, the prospect of greater tensions between her and Anne made Sam uneasy.

'You'd best be on your way then Kenny boy,' she said, gesturing towards the door. 'I understand Anne has a welcome for you.'
Kenny screwed his face up. 'What's that supposed to mean?'
'Both barrels,' Sam said. She held up her arms, pretending to hold a shotgun.
'Piss off,' Kenny said dismissively, but a second later, he betrayed a trace of uncertainty.
Sam saw it and pressed on. 'What kind of reception did you think you'd get Kenny? She's as mad as hell with you. You left her in the lurch to bring a child up by herself. All she has to do is contact the police and they'll be down on you like a ton of bricks.'
Kenny looked rattled.
'How many years is it without child support? Must be six by now. That's a lot of money you owe Kenny.'
'Eh?'
'You mean you didn't know?'

Kenny went silent. His eyes flicked back and forth, trying to process the information and the implications. Then he settled on: 'You really can't take a joke, can you?' He sneered in a weak attempt to gain the upper hand.
Sam raised both eyebrows. 'Not sure the law will see it that way, but maybe you know better, Kenny?'
Another cigarette found its way between his lips. 'Yeah, well maybe I do,' he said brazenly.

Dim as pitch, Sam thought. She knew he was on the ropes. 'Tell you what Kenny,' Sam said thoughtfully, 'How about I give you the bus fare out of here, and we'll keep this conversation to ourselves? If I see Anne, I'll tell her you were only here visiting the family.'
Kenny looked shifty-eyed. 'How much bus fare?'
'Forty quid,' Sam answered. The moment she said it, she could see he wanted more. She pressed the advantage before he had the chance to protest. 'And, there's no reason to inform the authorities you were ever here.'

He hesitated for a moment then held out his hand. Sam pulled out the money from her jeans pocket. She handed it to him then withdrew it at the last second. He looked into her stern eyes. 'But if I see you back here, I'll be first in line to grass you up.' She slapped the money in his hand, opened the door and averted her gaze. He sniffed, got up and made his way through the library. As he stepped onto the street he waved the money at Sam, stuck out his tongue, and walked off.

***

'I'd never have thought of that,' Anne said. She was in awe of Sam and utterly liberated by the knowledge Kenny was finally out of the picture. 'How did you know about him owing back money for child maintenance?'
'I didn't,' Sam said. 'I don't even know if it's true, but Kenny bought into it easily enough.'
'But how did the issue even come up?'
Sam brazened it out. 'I just asked him. We got chatting, so I asked if that's why he'd come back, to sort out your money. He looked pretty shocked when I said he must owe thousands. But the cherry on the cake was when I said I understood why.'
'Which was?' Anne asked wide-eyed.
'To avoid prison for evasion of child maintenance,' Sam grinned. 'I also mentioned you had a loaded shotgun as a welcome home present.'
Anne gasped, then fell about laughing from sheer relief.
Sam joined in. They hugged. It felt to Sam like they had reconnected. She gave her friend an extra squeeze.

***

Dom awoke, stiff-backed, but still feeling the heat from the sun on his body. He stood up, brushed some grass off his trousers and picked up his notepad. His hair stood on end when he looked down at it. Written in large, shaky, but perfectly eligible writing was one word: *Colby*.

13 A SECRET SHARED

Sam was continuing the process of emptying the shelves of books when her phone rang.

Dom was on the other end. He wanted to know whether she had any more information about the Old School House? He said he'd found what she'd dug out interesting, but wondered if there was anything about its time as a school.

Sam's initial reaction was that she didn't think so, but then she admitted that her first search for information had been fairly superficial. The big problem for her was time. She had access to various databases that maybe Dom didn't, but quite a lot of local history was in the form of old written documents. Most were piled haphazardly in the library store cupboard. Her quest had been to try and pull together what she could in one place and then digitalize the material in some coherent fashion.

She knew Dom must be familiar with historical research because of his background. If he was willing to wade through piles of dusty sheets he was welcome to.

It seemed a small price to pay and one Dom was happy to sign up to. He was eating at the *The Bomber* that evening and suggested they meet up: if she was able to bring more information, so much the better.

Dom was just finishing his meal when Sam approached his table. She was carrying two glasses of lager. Her torso tilted sideways, counterbalancing a heavy shoulder bag. Dom guessed they were documents.

'Something to wash it down,' she said, placing a glass in front of him. Dom didn't really care for lager, but he accepted graciously. 'I take it those are some papers for me to sift through?' He nodded towards the bag.

Sam dumped it down next to him and took the seat opposite. 'Some are on loan to me. Please put them back in the folders and don't lose any.'

'I promise,' said Dom.

'So, what's the interest in the Old School House?'

Dom provided a brief history of the house as it related to his wife, Alice. Sam already knew most of it, but she was attentive. Of greater interest to her was why he would want to buy the place. She knew from Anne that Alice had been interested in buying her childhood home, but surely, in the circumstances, he could have backed out? Maybe he didn't want to. Maybe it was a way of maintaining some connection with her. She remembered Anne's brief date with Dom. Anne had said his main interest in her was what she could remember about Alice. She realized she had stopped listening to him. He was looking back at her waiting for a response. So she nodded and said: 'I see.' He seemed satisfied.

Dom excused himself and headed to the bar to order more drinks. She quaffed the contents of her glass, realizing how thirsty she was. She still hadn't eaten and could feel the rapid effects of the alcohol. She gestured to Dom to get some snacks. He returned with a bag of crisps.

Dom could see she looked tired. He asked how she was and was met with a grunt. He pressed on, enquiring what was happening to the books, and to her.

'I've been told they don't have space for the books,' she answered. 'I'm supposed to give them away or ask for them to be disposed of.' Her eyes welled up at the prospect.

Dom didn't do well with emotions. He aimed for distraction. 'Well, you never know,' he said, trying to sound upbeat. 'Things turn up when you least expect it.'

Sam wasn't in the mood. She gave Dom the sort of withering look that said patronize me at your peril.

The booze was already making her feel disinhibited. She knew she was on the edge of saying something she might later regret and so changed the subject. 'How's your work coming along then?'

'Pretty good.'

Sam downed her drink and pointed to his glass.

Dom hadn't even started. He was startled at the speed Sam could put them away. He shook his head.

With each mouthful, Sam became more loquacious. The chattering became more personal. She asked Dom what his intentions were with Anne. He said he had none. She said that he should and pursed her lips, just in case what she'd said wasn't clear enough.

Dom began to feel uncomfortable. There was nothing worse than dealing with someone who was getting more and more drunk.

She began pointing to the people at the bar, talking loudly, saying which one's never used the library. Then she speculated about their preferred reading. Her comments were causing heads to turn. She was being met with raised eyebrows and expressions of mild irritation, but Dom sensed that could quickly change.

With the atmosphere souring, he pulled the bag of documents onto his lap, making moves that he was leaving.

Sam seemed not to notice. She had suddenly gone quiet. Her eyes were hooded, her head drooped and she stared dreamily at the table. 'I saw her you know, but nobody believed me,' she slurred.

Dom stood up, pulling the strap of the bag over his shoulder. 'We'll catch up sometime, Sam.' He took a couple of paces towards the exit and then felt guilty. He could hardly leave her slumped across the table. He turned back, crouched next to her and put her arm over his shoulder.

'Unhand me, you beast,' Sam mumbled, grinning to herself.

He pulled her up.

Realizing their height difference, he removed her arm from his shoulder and wrapped his own around her waist. They staggered out of the pub, critical eyes following them.

'You believe me, don't you, Dom?' She droned.

'Sure,' Dom answered, wondering what was best to do with her. 'Where do you live, Sam?'

She took mock offence and pulled away from him. 'Saucy,' she said, but she pointed the way and they lurched forward. 'She never spoke, never, never.'

'Who?' Dom asked. He had no particular interest in her ramblings but he wanted to keep her alert enough to walk. The prospect of her collapsing into a drunken heap wasn't an attractive one.

Sam raised her voice. 'Her. Alice Drew. Who do you think?' Then, 'why have we stopped?'
Dom felt his body stiffen. He turned to face her. 'What are you saying? You've seen Alice Drew?' His question came out with an intensity he hadn't planned.
It seemed to have a sobering effect. Sam's eyes focused on his for just a moment.
'Nope,' she answered, snorting with laughter.
It was hugely frustrating. He wasn't sure how much he would get out of Sam in this condition but he had to try. He lightened his tone. 'I hear she wore trousers all the time,' he said. It was the first thing to come to mind, which suddenly sounded very stupid.
They continued staggering forward.
Sam wagged a finger, 'No. A long dress and a white blouse.'
He felt his senses move to high alert.
'And she was tall,' he ventured.
She stooped forward and laughed. It was all Dom could do not to let her drop.
'What have you been reading? Her words were beginning to merge and become even less coherent. She sprang to attention and pushed out her hand, palm side down. 'This tall.'
It was everything he needed to know. If this was madness, he and Sam shared it. He felt a profound sense of relief.

***

Sam woke with a crashing headache and a stiff neck. Her tongue stuck to the roof of her mouth and her throat felt like sandpaper. She gradually got her bearings and realized she was on her sofa, covered with a duvet.
The memories of the previous evening were fractured but parts gradually assembled. She groaned with embarrassment.
A flash of panic followed as she tried to remember what day it was. Almost as quickly she slumped back, recalling it was her day off.

After a while she pulled off the duvet, only then realising Dom must have gone upstairs and removed it from her bed. Her bedroom was a mess and yet another reason to groan inwardly.

She sat up, head in hands, trying to make her eyes work. They were gritty and didn't seem to want to focus.

There was a jug of water, two aspirin, a glass and a note on the coffee table. She moved forwards, dropped down on one knee, and caught the note between her fingertips. She struggled to sit back on the sofa, alternating sighs with obscenities then opened the note:

Rehydrate. When you feel human again, give me a call.

She screwed the note into a ball and threw it to one side. A call. He was either desperate or he wanted to give her a piece of his mind. Some other time, she thought.

***

It was a tedious business. Dom had quickly worked his way through the papers that Sam categorized now he was left with what remained. Sheets were stuck together, either by age or uncertain means. Many were torn. Some were barely legible.

He had made a mental shortlist of things he considered might be relevant. Any references to the house or school were obvious, but back then the church would have kept its own records and these sometimes varied from Parish to Parish. Had Sam managed to acquire them? It was early days but he hadn't seen any in this batch.

He wondered whether he could give Sam a phone call. She might not be in the best frame of mind. Then he had a twinge of anxiety. He shouldn't be spending time on this he should be working on his own book. People were depending on him and he still needed to finalise.

He looked at the pile of papers in front of him and wondered just how much more Sam might have. Maybe he'd press on a little longer. What difference would another day make?

14 DISCLOSURE

The soft, dreamy tones, of Claire de Lune, entered Dom's dreams. He lay in bed, more asleep than awake, comforted by Debussy's gentle piano piece. Gradually, as he became more alert, he realised it was coming from downstairs, from his own piano.

It could only be Miss Drew. He remained still, apprehensive, wondering what his next move should be.

Then the message she'd left came to mind. That name, Colby; he needed to know more. What if she could only write?

He cursed under his breath. Why hadn't he left a notepad downstairs, or in the garden, or both?

He slipped out of bed, moving quietly, worried that any noise might cause her to disappear.

Reaching the top of the stairs he saw her, as real as any other person, sitting at the piano.

She looked up at him, continuing to play, her face tranquil and still.

He felt soothed by her presence.

Was this how it was meant to be, he wondered? A diet of horror films and campfire stories suggested otherwise, but they were just designed to shock, tapping into primal fears of the unknown.

But here, in her presence, it felt very different. All his earlier concerns had been fed by his own assumptions and sense of vulnerability. But now, there was no sense of her as intruding.

The music continued to waft around the house. He sat on the top stair and listened, fascinated by the apparition in front of his eyes. It felt like a rare privilege, a gift of sorts, to be allowed in her presence.

It was hard to think of Miss Drew as a ghost. The word itself was loaded with negative connotations. But what was better? Spectre, vision, spirit? They all felt wrong. And why should she be burdened with a label? She had once been a person, no different from anyone else. Who knew why some part of her was still here? The fact was, nobody really knew anything about the afterlife. Miss Drew could be just as perplexed.

He made a decision. No more talk of ghosts. She was Miss Drew in life - that was satisfactory now.

How many people had actually been in the presence of someone like her, he wondered? Maybe more than realised. If they were all like Miss Drew, they simply came and went. Maybe they looked a little different, a bit out of place, but they didn't float through walls, or appear as a mist, or hover in mid-air. They didn't set out to frighten.

There were so many questions about what it all meant.

Miss Drew stopped playing. She looked down at the piano and rested her hands on her lap.

Dom slowly stood up. 'You play beautifully, Miss Drew.'

She did not react.

He trod on a step. It snapped beneath his weight.

She was gone.

***

'If you think I'm going to be lectured to about the other night, you can think again,' Sam said forcefully.'

'That's not what I meant,' Dom answered. 'I just wanted to follow something up with you. Plus, I'd like to pick your brain about the papers you put my way.'

The phone went quiet as Sam calmed down.

She came back to him. 'That's alright then. What is it you want to know?'

'Can we meet, Sam? I've got a few things I'd like to talk about. How about my place for supper?'

'Are you chatting me up,' Sam asked, resorting to familiar repartee.

'If omelette and salad counts, then maybe I am.'

'So long as you don't expect me to eat radishes, I accept.'

'Excellent. Come straight from work if you can.'

Sam noticed how fidgety and preoccupied Dom looked over supper. They had gone over old ground about the library, the press release, the protest and had laughed. It was polite conversation but Sam sensed he was building to the bigger issue. She wasn't wrong.

'Sam, the other night in the pub,' he began.

'Oh come on,' she sounded deflated, 'you said you wouldn't.'

He cast a hand across his face as if to close it down. 'Something specific,' he continued. 'You mentioned that you had see Alice Drew.'

Sam looked back wide-eyed. 'I said that?'

'And I wanted to know if you could elaborate? That's all.'

A silence descended. Sam's expression gave little away – then she grinned self-consciously. 'If by elaborate you mean explain yourself, that's easy, I was talking drunken gibberish.' She raised her eyebrows and pulled her mouth down, tight-lipped.

Dom shook his head. 'No, it was more than that. You were drunk, but you weren't speaking gibberish. The booze had simply loosened up a memory you've been suppressing for years.'

Sam scoffed. 'Listen to you, Freud. I wasn't aware you were a part-time analyst.' She got up from the table and made her way to the piano. Trying to change subject she asked: 'do you play?'

'No. You're avoiding the question.'

She sat on the piano stool and flicked the sheet music. 'There's really nothing to say, Dom. When we were kids, we used to invent stories, people, places.' She met his eyes as he walked towards her. 'I guess I never grew up.'

This was getting nowhere, Dom thought. It was a risk but one he'd have to take. After all, it was just he and Sam here. 'I've seen her too,' he said quietly.

Sam laughed. 'Oh that's good. You think by saying that it'll get me to talk more about spooks.' She pressed a key on the piano. 'Wrong,' she sang, mimicking the note.

'I want to show you something,' Dom said, walking away from her and towards the mantelpiece.

Sam noted the seriousness with which he was speaking.

He returned with a notepad and placed it on the piano in front of her. She picked it up and blew between her lips. 'Colby. Did you write this? You must have held the pen between your teeth.'

'That's what I'm trying to tell you,' Dom said. 'Until I heard you say that about Alice Drew, I thought I was becoming unhinged.' He began pacing the room. It was the trigger for everything to spill out. 'She was here the first night I moved in. She was actually studying one of the monitors being used by those ghost hunter people. I saw her, as clearly as I can see you. I thought she was with them. Then she was in the garden and the other day she was actually playing this very piano.'

Sam stood up and chose to sit somewhere else.

'This,' Dom grabbed the notepad and waved it around, 'was left for me in the garden.'

'Anyone could have written that,' Sam said.

'No they couldn't. I was alone. I drifted off for just a few moments and when I looked at the notepad, there it was.'

Sam crossed her legs and began scratching her ankle. 'So who, or what, is Colby anyway?'

'Exactly,' Dom exclaimed, throwing his arms wide. 'That's why I asked you here. Not only have you seen Alice Drew, you're also the local historian and librarian. If anyone knows the history of this place, it's you.'

Sam showed him the palm of her hand and shook her head. 'Go slow, Dom. I can certainly try to find out more about the house, but don't you think the talk about ghosts is stretching credulity somewhat?'

Dom looked hurt and betrayed. He walked over to the sofa and slumped down. He sighed melancholically. 'I've opened up to you, Sam. I thought the one person who would understand and could help me make sense of all this, would be you.'

Sam remained quiet. She was left looking at the top of his head as he slouched forward, arms on knees. She couldn't bring herself to say the words he wanted to hear, but she didn't want to betray his trust. Then, that same pained expression she had seen before began looking back at her. She got up, sat next to Dom and cupped his hands.

'I know how to keep my mouth shut,' she said earnestly, 'and I want to help you, but . .'

Dom over-talked her. 'But you'd prefer to find a reason not to,' he said sharply. He pulled his hands away.

'Actually, if you'd let me finish, I was going to say, but I still have an issue with time. This is the first evening I've taken time off in about three weeks.'

'So, what then? Where does that leave us?'

Sam stood up. 'Come with me. I'll show you something.'

It was early evening and still warm. Dom asked what was happening, but Sam maintained it was easier if he saw for himself.

They reached the library a few minutes later. Sam unlocked the door, switched on the lights and led him to a side door. She punched in a number code, opened up and switched on the light. 'After you.' She moved to one side.

Dom stepped into a small room. He was surrounded by rows of shelving running from top to bottom. Every shelf was filled with boxes, files and stacks of paper, bound with ribbon or string.

'This,' Sam said, 'is what I loosely describe as our local history archive. Actually it's a chaotic pile of records dating back to goodness knows when. Over the years, a lot of it has been moved from building to building, ending up here. I suspect most of it could be burned.'

'There must be weeks of work in here,' Dom said.

'Maybe. Although, I've sifted through about half as much again. As I say, most of it was dross, but anything that had a shred of interest or bearing on local history, I've kept. I dropped off a sample for you to look at.'

Dom conceded defeat. 'I see what you mean, Sam. I'm sorry, I really had no idea.'

Sam turned off the light and closed the door. 'Thing is, Dom, the library is closing soon. These papers have to be stored somewhere or they'll simply be disposed of. You're welcome to spend your time trawling through, but you won't have much time.'

A thought struck him. 'That barn at the back of my house; it's dry and it's empty. Could we use that as storage?'

Sam shrugged. 'It's quite a modern barn isn't it. So yes, that's a good idea. There's a couple of lads in the village with a van. They'll shift the lot and they won't charge much.'

Dom clapped his hands together. 'Give me their number and I'll sort it out.'

They left together and Sam locked up. Dom asked whether she'd like to come back to continue the evening, but she declined.

He nodded, turned to leave, then felt her hand on his arm. When he looked to see what she wanted, he was met with an anxious look.

'I've done you a disservice,' she said. She looked up and down the street to see if anyone was in earshot. 'You were honest with me about Alice Drew and I wasn't straight with you.'

'You mean?'

'Yes. I really did see her. Several times actually.'

Dom placed his hands on her arms and gave a gentle squeeze. He radiated gratitude. 'Thank you, Sam.' He could see it wasn't easy for her and he understood why. Suppress a secret for long enough and it eventually leads to denial. 'Let's start again,' he said.

15 ANOTHER PIECE OF THE PUZZLE

Millie gave Sam a big wave. She was feeding the calf with a bottle and didn't want to stop. Sam called over that she'd brought a couple of books for her.
Millie's face fell a shade. She liked books, up to a point, but they weren't real presents.
Sam pretended not to notice and stepped into Anne's always-open door. She produced a bottle of wine.
In the way that only comes with long-term friendships, the pair didn't often bother with hellos and goodbyes. The gaps in their companionship were as natural as the time spent in each other's company.
'Bit early for that,' Anne said.
Sam put the bottle on the table. 'Alright, I can wait a few minutes longer.'

Anne pulled a couple of dinner plates down from the rack and said it was a good excuse for an early lunch. She quickly assembled a familiar cold plate of cheese, pickle, bread and apple. Sam popped the cork and poured some into two tumblers.
Millie came running in and gave Sam a big hug.
Sam ruffled her hair and insisted she was growing faster than any six-year old she knew.
Millie looked delighted and stretched herself to look even taller.
Times like this made Sam feel she was missing something in her life.
Millie was such a delightful kid. She could only imagine what it must be like to have a mother's attachment.

'Go wash your hands,' Anne said, 'and you can take your sandwich and watch a little television.'

It was a rare treat to watch cartoons during the day. She did as she was bid, grabbed her lunch and left the friends alone.

Anne said: 'What news?'

'Same old,' Sam replied. 'If I fill another skip with books I think I'll throw up. It's back breaking. Not to mention heart breaking.'

'Have you sorted out where they're going?'

Sam shook her head and nibbled on some cheese. 'Well, there's no way I can give them all away. And I'm even struggling to think about it. They're meant to be a shared resource.'

Despite the casual language, Anne could see her friend was upset. She was about to change topic when Sam continued.

'The good news is that Dominic Ross has volunteered to house the local history archives in his barn.'

Anne gave Sam an interested look. She wondered how she had pulled that off. The pair had obviously been talking.   .

Sam, however, was interested in other things. She traced a finger around the edge of her plate. 'You remember when we were kids, playing at the Old School House?' She looked furtively at Anne, 'did you ever imagine seeing things there?'

It triggered Anne's memory. 'Oh yes. You remember that old lamp that used to be outside?'

Sam nodded.

'Well it used to cast a shadow on the trees opposite. I thought it looked like a huge snake.'

'You never mentioned.'

'Maybe I was too scared. Anyway, why do you ask?'

Sam took a sip of wine. 'Oh no reason. I suppose it was the offer of the barn that got me thinking about the old place.'

Anne said: 'Did you find it creepy?'

'Never.'

'Me neither. Not the house. Alice's folks were always so welcoming.'

'I guess that's why Alice was keen to come back. Happy memories and all that.'

The two went quiet, lost in their own brief memories of Alice, their childhood friend.'

Anne broke the spell. 'Alice's mum once told me when Alice was born they still hadn't settled on a name for her.'

Sam looked up. 'Oh?'

'Her name came from a scrap of paper they found with the name Alice scrawled on.' Anne caught Sam's expression. 'You alright? You look like someone just walked over your grave.'

Sam smiled uneasily and necked her wine back.

'Go steady, it's only lunchtime,' Anne frowned.

Sam stared into the middle distance, lost in thought. She became aware of Anne studying her. She affected a business like manner. 'Talking of scraps of paper, the reason I stopped by, was to ask if you fancied doing some hard labour? Specifically, paper checking.'

'Meaning?'

'It's some project Dominic is involved with. He's trying to find out more about the history of the Old School House.'

Anne bit into her apple and chewed thoughtfully. 'I don't see why I should use what free time I have volunteering for that. If he's so keen why doesn't he pay for some helpers?'

It was a good idea and one Sam capitalised on. 'He is, paying I mean.'

Anne showed interest. 'Tell me more.'

'I don't know the details,' Sam said. 'I just wondered if you might be interested, that's all.' She felt Anne's wary eyes on her.

'Extra cash is always welcome. I suppose I could pitch in on the days Terry helps out. What's involved.'

Sam shrugged. She'd got away with the lie and began to relax. 'I'll ask. And I'll find out what he's paying.' She bit off a generous piece of cheese and topped up her glass.

***

'Absolutely not,' Dom protested. 'I haven't got money to pay for an assistant.'

Sam gave him a hard stare. 'You can't have it all ways. How do you expect to find out about – you know who – if you don't put some work in?' She gave a calculating look. 'You could be using that time to focus on your own work.' By the look on his face she could tell she'd touched a nerve.

He sighed and took a sip of beer. 'How much then?'

Sam raised an eyebrow. 'An assistant doing basic admin – say twenty an hour?'

Dom thought for a moment then shook his head. 'Ten.'

'Fifteen. She won't turn out for less and I wouldn't blame her.'

He shifted uneasily in his seat. 'Fifteen then. But I want to see results.' He reached for his wallet and took out three twenty-pound notes. 'Let's see how far this gets me and I'll consider offering more if I'm impressed.'

Sam reached over and took the money. 'You've got yourself an assistant. And there's more.' She leaned across the table and stole a chip from his plate.

'Get your own,' he moaned.

'Why are men so possessive about chips?'

'It's because women don't order them and steal off our plates.' He pulled his plate an inch nearer himself. 'What do you mean there's more?'

'You mustn't get upset,' she said studying Dom, 'it's not anything weird or nasty, but I am going to mention something about your Alice, which is,' she looked cautiously around the pub for eavesdroppers, and forced a whisper, 'relevant.'

He stopped eating, frowned at her and said: 'go on.'

Sam reported the conversation she'd had with Anne over how Alice got her name. 'Don't you see, another note?'

Dom pursed his lips thoughtfully. 'I'm not upset,' he said. 'In fact this whole issue has thrown into doubt all my assumptions about life and death. I've moved to a state of open-mindedness.' He got up from his chair and moved around to be closer to Sam. He leaned in to speak quietly to her. 'If this means what we think it means, Miss Drew is not only able to write, she's actively listening to what people say.'

Sam nodded. 'But how does that help us?'

'No idea. But it's a step forward. We've revealed another piece of the puzzle.'

Back at the farm, Sam told Anne the news and passed over the money. 'That's great, I'd have done it for ten an hour.' Anne looked pleased.

'Don't ever tell him that,' Sam said. 'In fact, you should complain about slave labour when you see him. Before you start, I'll give you a list of the things to look out for and a method to store and record the findings. It's a doddle.'

'You're a pal.'

Sam smiled and tipped her head to one side. 'Are you going to eat that sandwich?'

'Help yourself.'

As Sam tucked in, Anne used the opportunity to find out more about Sam and Dom. 'Have you been seeing a lot of Dominic recently?'

Sam's radar flickered into life. She casually continued to enjoy her snack. 'A bit, I suppose. He dropped by to ask about the Old School House and I showed him the store full of papers.'

'Anything more than that?'

Sam sighed heavily as she threw a critical stare at her friend. 'We're not going down that road again, are we? I told you, he's not interested, I'm not interested.'

Anne met the look and pulled a face.

'Oh, alright. I wouldn't say no, but he's not interested in me, Annie. I've told you that already.' Sam decided it was time to give some back.

'Anyway, if you're so interested in him why haven't you done something about it?'

'Who says I am? Look the guy lost his wife just over a year ago. He's probably not even thinking about dating.'

'Not that you'd know.'

Anne raised her voice. 'What's that supposed to mean?'

'It means, you can't hide behind a herd of cows and pretend you know what he's thinking.'

Anne looked deflated. 'I don't think I know what that means.'

Sam's irritation changed to sympathy. 'It means you're hiding yourself away. You say you'll do things but nothing actually changes. You constantly use the farm as the excuse for doing nothing.'

Anne turned her back to Sam and looked out of the window. 'Well, maybe I'm happy this way.'

Sam stood joined her friend and hooked arms. She spoke softly. 'And maybe I'm often mistaken for Audrey Hepburn.'

16 THE FIRE

Anne was hesitant on the phone. 'Anyway, it's a big chicken and a big apple pie, so if you'd like to join us for Sunday lunch, you'd be very welcome. Plus, it will make up a little for the evening I cut short.'
Dom leaned back, averting his eyes from his computer screen. 'Well, I do have to eat, and a home cooked Sunday roast certainly beats another meal at *The Bomber*.' He hesitated, wondering if there was anything else behind the offer. He wasn't sure he wanted to get drawn into a relationship with Anne.
'And there's a few more things I can show you from the work I'm doing for you.'
That was it. She was probably hoping for more work. He relaxed a little. 'Sounds great, I'll see you then.'

Anne put down the phone and examined her feelings. Yes, he was a good-looking guy. He was pleasant company and he was great with Millie. But she had to admit to a lack of buzz. Maybe it was the fact she was out of practice? Or, maybe Sam's comments had put her under pressure. Still, at the end of the day it was only Sunday lunch and there were a couple of things she could show him that related to his interest in the Old School House. She pulled on her coat. It was time to do a food shop.

'About time,' Sam said, popping open the biscuit tin. 'Why lunch and not dinner?'

Anne took a digestive and dipped its edge in her tea. 'I thought it was more informal. I didn't want to build any expectations. Get to know each other – you know?'

Sam was all too familiar with Anne's caution. She was a soft target in that regard, but today she felt supportive. 'Good plan,' she said. 'What's in your bag?'

'Chicken, snacks, bottle of white.' Anne looked around the library. 'Looks like you've finished.'

'Pretty much. It's decision time with the books though.' She scratched her head and screwed up her face. 'Only I can't decide.' She leaned heavily on the table. 'There's been a bit of cherry picking. All the DVD's and CD's have gone and some of the more popular titles, but that still leaves hundreds of books.'

Anne rattled the biscuit tin. 'Go on, you know it'll help.'

Sam dipped her hand in. 'Well, it can't make things worse.'

***

Dom was punctual. He'd brought a potted plant, a bottle of wine and a chocolate egg with a toy for Millie. 'Smells fantastic,' he said, stepping into the kitchen.

'There's a bottle chilling in the fridge, if you'd like to do the honours,' Anne replied. She noticed they were both wearing the same outfit of cashmere jersey and jeans.

Millie wandered in, her hands behind her back. She gave Dom a big cheeky smile.

'Got something for you,' Dom said, 'but you'll have to eat it when mum says.'

A loud parp filled the kitchen. Millie produced the clown horn from behind her back. Both she and Dom laughed, but the noise had caught Anne by surprise. She had cried out at the noise and had her hand on her chest looking shocked. Millie could barely maintain her balance for laughing, which made Dom laugh even more.

Anne scowled accusingly at Dom and turned away.

Millie and Dom shared a silent face-pulling moment before Millie declared she wanted to check on the calf. She ran off to the sound of Anne telling her not to get dirty.

The meal went well. The adults moved into the lounge while Millie went upstairs to play in her bedroom.

'You make a cracking apple pie,' Dom said, relaxing into a chair.

'Mum's recipe.'

'Of course.' He watched as Anne sifted through a few papers. She pulled one out and checked it.

'I thought this was interesting,' she said. 'It's a newspaper clipping. It's quite fragile, so I put it in this plastic sleeve.' She passed it to Dom.

It was a news report on the school fire. The headline stated: *Drunken Blunder Costs Daughter's Life*. Dom couldn't contain his surprise. He gasped: 'this is astonishing,' he rapidly scanned the piece, searching for the key information. 'Have you read it?'

Anne sat opposite Dom, sipping wine. 'You might need to borrow my magnifying glass, it's hard to read in places.'

'What's the gist?'

'The teacher's dad was the caretaker. He had the job of feeding the stove and they reckon he forgot to shut the panel. A hot coal fell out and, well, we know the rest.'

'He was drunk?'

'You've seen the headline.'

He shook his head. 'Can you imagine, living with that on your conscience?'

Anne automatically looked up to where Millie was playing. 'No, I really can't.'

'Does it say anything else?'

'Well, it says all the children got out safely. There's also a bit about the tragedy of the teacher who lost her life searching for a child who was safely outside.'

Dom flicked the paper with his finger. 'This is excellent, Anne. Is there much more left to do?'

'I've got a few more box files to work through. I'm getting quicker.'

'And am I still in credit?' He reached towards his back pocket for his wallet.

She raised a hand. 'We're good. I'll let you know if and when.'

Millie came downstairs and paid some attention to Dom, showing him her favourite dolls. She said they had lots of clothes and one even had a horse to ride. Dom said he'd like to see that, so Millie clambered her way back upstairs.

'She's lovely,' Dom said, following her progress.

'Why did you move here?' Anne asked. It sounded blunt, but it was out there.

Dom didn't seem offended. He smiled knowingly. 'Well, as I recall, you had quite a hand in that.'

'Yes but,' she couldn't find the right words.

'But that was before Alice died, you mean?'

She was pleased that Dom chose to run with it. 'Well, yes.'

Had Anne asked that question just a few weeks ago he would have told her to mind her own business. Now, none of that seemed to matter. 'I suppose it was a way of keeping contact with her,' he said. 'She was so happy when you let her know about the house being up for sale.'

'Has it helped?'

'Yes actually, but not in ways I'd expected.'

It was a puzzling comment but Anne didn't want to pry too much. 'I'm pleased,' she said.

Millie ran in. Her doll was dressed in riding gear and was sitting on a brown pony. Dom spent a while admiring it. He wondered whether Millie could do a drawing of them for him. As an incentive he took a pound coin from his pocket. She didn't seem terribly impressed by the coin but said she had lots of crayons and headed back upstairs.

Anne changed topic. 'I was thinking about something Sam said. She's desperately unhappy that the book stock is likely to be destroyed.'

'I know,' Dom frowned and nodded in sympathy.

'So, I wondered if you could help?'

Dom met Anne's gaze. 'How exactly?'

'Your barn. It's huge and unless you've got plans, it would be a great place to store all the books until she can decide what to do with them.'

He looked uncomfortable. 'And what if she can't? I'd have a barn stuffed full of old books.'

Anne chewed the side of her mouth nervously. 'But you're an author. Isn't there someone you know that could help out?'

'No. Because what you're talking about is the distribution or disposal of a load of well-thumbed old books. I think Sam already knows the options.'

'She's so upset. She'll be without a job too.'

'I didn't know that,' Dom said. He could feel himself rapidly relenting. 'Look, if you think it will help soften the blow, she can use the barn.'

***

'That's a real find,' Sam said, referring to Anne's discovery.

'My heart goes out to the father,' Dom added. 'Can you imagine the guilt?'

Sam agreed. 'And having to live it down in a small village like this, it would be hard enough today.'

Dom tucked the phone under his chin and stirred soup on the stove. 'The thing is, does it move us any further forward?'

'Well, I suppose we know more than we did before, but as for explaining Alice Drew, no it doesn't.' Anne is still sifting through the paperwork, so she might turn up more.'

'How was your lunch?'

'Oh, you know about that?'

'I know many things.'

Dom smiled. 'Do you know what *I'm* having for lunch?

'Yes.'

'Go on then, tell me.'

Sam put on her haughty voice. 'No. because unlike you, I have work to do.' She hung up, biting her bottom lip and wondering if she'd upset him.

Once the surprise of being hung up passed, Dom found himself grinning like a schoolboy in a sweet shop. He really liked Sam and he was starting to think of her as something more than a friend. He was on the edge of phoning her back but changed his mind. His soup was ready. He sent a text: *barn is available for book storage – let me know.*

Seconds later his phone pinged: *you adorable man. See you in the barn,* followed by a winking emoji.

17 PROGRESS AND IMPASSE

His phone trilled. Dom looked at the display panel and saw the name of his agent, India Morley. He paused for a moment then snatched the phone from its cradle. It was make or break time. He put on his cheery voice: 'India, good of you to call.'

India's voice was husky from years of smoking. 'I knew you could do it, dear boy.'

Dom felt the tension leave his neck and shoulders. 'I'm pleased you like it,' he said, attempting to sound more relaxed than he felt, 'still just a rough draft of course.'

'But good enough for the backers,' she said. 'They know the quality of your work and they'll understand this is work in progress. But that's the key word – progress.'

'Good news all round then,' Dom said.

'Now we need to do some glad-handing and back-patting,' India went on. Her voice adopted the husky suggestive quality she used when she wanted something from men. Thirty years ago it might have come across as sensual, but now it sounded a little disturbing 'How do you fancy hosting it at your place? Our American backers will love all that rustic charm.'

Dom's stomach hit the floorboards. His home was a retreat, not a party venue. 'You've been here, India. You know what the roads are like,' he protested.

A gritty laugh came down the line. 'My dear, they'll be coming by private jet and helicopter. My team will rustle up a patch of concrete nearby. Norfolk is full of old airfields.' She bulldozed her way through his reluctance. 'Leave everything to me, sweetheart. One of mine will contact you with the details. Oh, and you should invite local people too. It shows how grounded and accessible you are. If you can't find any, let me know.' Before he could say another word, the line went dead.

Moments later, it rang again. He attempted to stiffen his resolve. It was Sam. 'Oh, it's you,' he muttered.

'Charming. Hello to you too,' she said.

'Sorry, I thought you were my agent again. What's up?'

'What's up is yet more information.' Her enthusiasm was building. 'I figured I'd do a little research into births, marriages and deaths and guess what?'

'Guessing, can't imagine,' Dom sighed.

'Albert Drew, Alice's father, committed suicide a few months after the fire.'

A silence followed as Dom processed the information.

'You still there, Dom?'

'Sorry, yes. I mean that's really interesting, and very sad, but I'm just thinking.'

'What?'

'Well, how does any of this help us with Alice? I'm not sure where it's all leading, or what we do with the information. We're assuming it will give us some insight into why Alice Drew is here, but will it?

It was an observation Sam was willing to concede. 'I've been thinking along the same lines,' Sam said. 'Say we pulled together absolutely all there is to know, then what?'

'I haven't seen or heard from her for quite a while, you know.'

Another pause.

Sam said: 'we do need another strategy. Meanwhile, there's no harm pressing on with fact finding.'

In the absence of an alternative it felt like movement. 'Sure. What's next?'

'I don't know if it will lead anywhere but I'm trying to track what happened to young Master Colby. After all, he was the one Alice Drew ran back into the building to save.'

'True, but he was actually outside the school all along. I can't see that getting us anywhere.'

'Look, I have to go. We may have to concede the fact that all of this will get us nowhere. Anyway, speak to you soon.' She hung up.

The thought that this particular approach to Alice Drew might reveal nothing didn't trouble Dom. She had been here a long time and so long as she was able to leave messages, there was every chance she would communicate again.

But that troubled him. His work had been a useful distraction. Even the research into Alice Drew had provided something for his mind to focus on. His depth of grief was slowly diminishing and this seemed to correspond with fewer appearances by Miss Drew. Quite what that meant for understanding her needs, or her motives, was uncertain.

He picked up his notepad. In large letters he wrote: Albert Drew, drunk, caused fire. He took it downstairs and laid it on the piano keyboard.

**

It took three visits by a large container lorry to move the books from the library into the barn. When it was done, the barn was filled with wheeled skips, stuffed to the brim with books.

Sam and Dom stood by the door, assessing the effect.

'That library was like the Tardis,' Dom said, 'are you sure you haven't sneaked in a load from other places?'

Sam nudged him in the side. 'It's what barns are for,' she said. She looked him up and down, and spoke suggestively: 'unless you know of other uses them?' Her phone made a noise.

Dom said: 'saved by the ping.'

Sam's expression tightened as she began to read.

'Bad news?'

She pushed the phone into her jeans pocket, looking perplexed. 'Not sure what to make of this but my source informs me that young Master Colby was a naughty boy.'

'How so?'

'He had a police record – for arson.'

They retreated into the house to take stock. Dom said if Miss Drew could listen to conversations, this was one he'd like her to hear.

Sam looked sceptical, but it made little difference to her. Part of her thought all this was an interesting distraction, but she'd begun to wonder if Dom was using it as an excuse to keep seeing her.

They sat on the sofa, their knees angled towards one another.

'So, this shines a new light on what might have happened,' Dom began. 'Let's accept Miss Drew's dad liked a tipple. The newspaper reported as much but we're talking Edwardian times. Most working men would be drinking beer as a matter of course.'

'And he probably had a work routine, and a limited amount of money to spend, like most men,' suggested Sam.

'People would have looked for a reason to blame,' Dom continued. 'Miss Drew's father shovelled coal into the stove, so he was responsible. Maybe some spiteful neighbour reported he spent his lunch break in the pub. Why would anyone even consider it was one of the children?'

Sam edged a little further towards Dom. Their knees touched. 'And young Colby was missing from the head count when Alice Drew got them outside. It's why she ran back inside the burning school.'

'Only he somehow turned up with the other children. Could he have left by a different exit?'

A loud noise, like a slap, made them both jump.

'What the.' Sam grabbed the seat of the sofa and looked towards the source of the noise.

Dom sprang up and stood rigid.

They looked at the notepad he had left on the piano. It appeared to stick against the nearby wall, then drop to the ground.

Sam jumped up next to Dom and grabbed his arm. 'Was that?'

Dom felt his heart thumping in his chest. 'Maybe.'

'Too much,' Sam shouted. Her voice had jumped an octave. She stumbled to one side and began heading to the door.

Dom grabbed her. 'No wait,' he said. 'We're jumpy because it surprised us. She isn't out to harm us.'

Sam wriggled and tried to pull away. She looked terrified.

Without thinking, Dom used his strength and pulled her towards him. He folded her in his arms and held tight. 'You saw her as a child. She loves children. She's had ample opportunity to make my life a misery, but if anything I feel better when she's here.' He could feel the tension slowly start to leave Sam's body. He relaxed his grip. 'Let's just take a look at the notepad.'

They clung to one another as they approached the notepad. Dom let go of Sam and bent down to examine it. 'Nothing,' he said. 'No writing.'

Sam's composure began to return. 'I guess our conversation touched a nerve though.'

'Or something I'd written had.' He showed her his note.

'You wrote her dad was a drunk!' Sam shrieked. 'No wonder she flipped.'

'I didn't mean it that way,' Dom grumbled. 'It was a way of saying I understood what had happened.'

'Oh, subtle. And from what we've just found out, quite possibly wrong.' Sam ripped the page out of the pad and screwed it up. 'I think we're out of our depth.'

'I agree. But what do we do?'

Sam clasped his hand in both of hers. She liked the physical contact they'd just enjoyed, despite the circumstances. He didn't resist. 'Now don't freak, but maybe we should take Harry Wells into our confidence. I know he comes across as a bit geeky, but honestly, if you'd seen the books he's borrowed over the years. His knowledge is encyclopaedic.'

'The ghost hunter guy?' Dom said incredulously. 'I know nothing about him. It could be all over the Internet in five minutes.'

Sam led him back to the sofa. They coordinated sitting down. 'That's just his hobby,' she said. 'He takes it seriously but his day job is with Social Services. He's well used to keeping confidences.'

'Yes, but he's not obliged to do so here,' Dom said sullenly.

Sam stroked the back of his hand. 'You trusted me, Dom. Maybe you should extend that trust, or we'll end up going around in circles.'

18 HARRY

Harry Wells had a tear in his eye. He looked dazed, but with just the trace of a smile on his lips.

Dom and Sam looked at each other. They had just finished the story of Alice Drew and were trying to judge Harry's reaction. Dom was especially uneasy. He had put his faith in Sam's suggestion, so now it was down to whether he could trust Harry. The full implication of this getting out could have a devastating effect on his credibility as a writer. It was something he hoped he would never have to confront. But looking at Harry, he began to have his doubts. The man looked dishevelled. His double chin needed shaving, his shirt was out of his trousers and he wore odd socks. How did he get by in Social Services, Dom wondered, or were they all like this?

'I've waited my entire adult life for this moment,' Harry eventually said.

'So you believe the story,' Dom asked, even though he was certain of the answer.

Harry had Dom's notepad in his hand. He rested his fingers on the scrawl left by Alice Drew. 'Yes, I do,' he said dreamily.

Sam spoke up. 'So we wondered what to do next, Harry? Do you have any thoughts you could share?'

Harry looked bemused. 'Me? No, I don't think so.'

The sound of Dom's moan followed. 'What is the point?' He flopped back into the chair and covered his face with his hands.

Sam looked concerned. She had encouraged Dom to speak to Harry and it was already looking like a bad idea. She tried to encourage Harry to think. 'What about all those books you borrowed over the years? Haven't you come across anything like this?'

Harry took a swig from the bottle of beer Dom had provided. 'Well, there's nothing definitive,' he said. 'You have to appreciate that a lot stuff is first person accounts, or stories passed down. Hard to prove in other words.'

Harry was about to take another swig when something came to mind. It related to a coalmining incident in Wales that claimed the life of a young boy. For years after, miners told the story of a young boy who appeared with a lamp that had an unnatural glow. It wasn't uncommon for new boys down the mine to have tricks played on them. Typically, they'd be left alone in a pitch-black shaft while their companion, usually an older boy, took the lamp and pretended they needed to collect something. This usually lasted no more than a few minutes. But on this occasion, when the companion went back, the boy had disappeared, and they never found him.

'That's terrible,' Sam said, 'how old was the little boy?'

'Ten I expect,' Harry said. 'But the upshot was the companion was blamed and his family were shunned. In time, they had to move out of the village.'

'But I suppose he was to blame,' Dom said, joining the conversation. 'If he'd remembered where he'd left the poor lad, none of that would have happened. But I also can't see how that helps us.'

Harry casually crossed a leg and laid his palms on the arms of his chair. He looked like an overweight Abe Lincoln statue. 'That's cos' I haven't finished yet,' he said pithily.

'Well excuse me,' Dom muttered. He felt something jab his side and turned to see Sam's withering stare and stabbing finger.

'You see,' Harry continued, 'the companion always maintained his innocence. He also voiced suspicions about another lad called Tomas Morgan, who was always getting the boys into trouble. People did notice that Morgan became very subdued after the disappearance of the little boy, but nobody could prove anything, and I'm not sure they even tried.'

Sam became animated. 'Oh, I see the parallels. Someone is wrongly blamed and the real culprit gets away with it.'

Harry smiled. 'You're catching on.'

'And the spirit, or whatever we want to call it, remains in a state of limbo.' Sam looked pleased with herself.

'I don't want to be the fly in the ointment here,' Dom interjected, 'but think of all the countless times similar, or worse miscarriages, have affected people. The world should be full of lost souls. But it isn't.'
Harry shrugged. 'Who says it isn't? Our awareness of such phenomena is based around our own preconceptions and beliefs. And, dare I say it Mr Ross, our mental state at a particular point in time.'
'I don't mind you saying it, but your story suggests a little boy appeared to various miners who had nothing to do with the incident. Miss Drew is quite specific to me.'
Harry frowned and tapped his beer bottle with his fingernails. 'But Sam says she saw Alice Drew when she was a little girl.'
Dom had to concede the point. 'Fine, but I just don't get it. Why some and not others?'
'You said your own connection to Alice Drew began as a result of the grief you experienced,' Harry observed. 'And Sam, had something happened in your life when you saw Alice Drew?'
Sam looked at them both sheepishly. 'Well, I suppose it *may* have been around the time my father died. But honestly, I need to check the dates.'
Harry lifted his hands in a gesture of *case solved*.

Dom sighed deeply. 'The situations are not consistent and we're no further forward.'
'Well, we may be,' Harry said cautiously. 'They say the boy with the lamp stopped appearing after a confessional.'
Dom stroked his chin. 'Meaning?'
'On Tomas Morgan's deathbed, he confessed to his family that he was responsible. Basically he'd moved the new boy to the adjoining shaft. He thought it would be funny watching the lads scurry about trying to find him. But the shaft he moved him to wasn't safe. It was full of fissures and wasn't being worked any more. Chances are the lad tried to find a way out, or just stumbled, and fell into one.'
'What a fool,' Sam said. 'He destroys lives and only clears his conscience when he's about to die. Very helpful. But how does that link to the boy with the lamp no longer appearing?'

'His son was a lay preacher. He chose to tell the congregation at his father's funeral. After that, nobody ever reported seeing the boy with the lamp.'

The room fell silent. Dom and Sam spent time concentrating on each other's expressions.
'I wonder if you're thinking what I'm thinking,' Dom said.
'You mean a confessional? But we don't have the proof?'
'Not yet,' Dom said, 'but I wonder if we might obtain it?'
Harry pitched in. 'Ah, you're wondering if the living relatives of young Master Colby might be holding on to a secret?'
'That's exactly what I'm wondering,' Dom answered. 'So now we need to find if they exist and whether any are still in the village.'
'Parish records,' Sam said. 'They'll be a good place to start. Newer records will be data-based.'

Harry gave a heavy tired sigh. 'Well, I suppose I'd best be on my way. I hope I haven't taken you on a wild goose chase. As I say, these accounts aren't exactly reliable.' He grunted as he shifted his heavy bulk out of the chair and reached for his jacket.
Sam looked at Dom then nodded in Harry's direction.
Harry pulled on his jacket and offered his hand to Dom. 'Well, good luck, anyway.'
Dom shook his hand and felt magnanimous. 'Why don't you stay involved, Harry? We could use a consultant on the team.'
Harry beamed. 'It's Christmas come early,' he said. He gripped Dom's hand firmly. 'And don't worry, not a word of this will pass my lips.'
Dom looked solemn. 'I really do appreciate that, Harry. I hope that includes Tom and Dick, I know you share similar interests. The more people involved, the more likely this turns sour.'
Harry patted his hand. 'You have my word.'

As Harry stepped out of the door, Dom asked: 'How did you get involved in this sort of thing, Harry?'
'It was after the death of my boy. Motorcycle accident. I suppose I needed to know if there was more.' He rubbed his hands and smiled. 'And now I do.'

19 BRAD PITT

Guests were starting to arrive. The tiny village car park was already full and traffic lined the narrow country roads. Dom hoped his open invitation to villagers would quell potential unrest.

A jazz quartet struck up a gentle beat. The organisers had done well and despite his reservations, Dom was impressed.

His agent, India Morley, sidled up. Since the backers for the television series had turned on the money tap, she was a woman transformed. In fact, she was so delighted she decided this was a good time to drop her forty a day habit and turn to vaping. She took a puff and looked at the device with an expression bordering on contempt. 'You've taken the countryside to heart I see.' She had a view on fashion, which didn't include the jeans and sports jacket Dom was wearing.

'I love it here,' Dom said. 'You can breathe great gulps of air without worrying about car exhausts.'

She rolled her eyes. 'God,' she sighed, 'I'd kill for an exhaust emission right now.' She spotted someone significant and detached herself.

Dom spotted Anne, Sam and Millie coming up the drive. Anne looked stunning, walking like a ballerina and turning heads. Sam looked good too. She didn't carry herself in the effortless manner Anne did, but she had a way about her that captivated him. He became conscious of the fact he was staring at her and she'd noticed.

She flashed a knowing smile that had the effect of making his stomach tighten.

Millie was attracting attention by making parping sounds with her horn. She linked up with other children from the village and they began running around the bushes.

India cast a critical eye at Millie before looking to see if the noise was troubling the jazz quartet. They played on regardless.

Anne went off to organise a drink and snack for Millie while Sam made a beeline for Dom.

'Hello you,' he smiled.

She gave him a big hug, which caused him to look about self-consciously.

'Don't be coy,' Sam chastised, 'I've seen enough of those looks in my time to know what you were thinking; you dog.'

She'd caught him off balance but he quickly regained his composure. 'What do think?' He swept a hand around the assembly.

'Very nice,' Sam said. She loosened her grip and began looking more carefully at the guests. 'Who's that?' She nodded towards India.

'She's my agent,' Dom answered, 'more of a super-agent really. She moves and shakes and organises events like this.' He watched as India adjusted a strand of hair. She always struck him as the living embodiment of geometric design, in the way some people appear athletic, or pugilistic. She reminded him of the images on old Eastern European propaganda posters. Her hair had never changed from a severe bob cut in all the years he'd know her. Her face was angular, the tip of her chin chiselled, her cheekbones prominent. Today she was wearing a shapeless box of a blue jacket over white baggy trousers.

'She's striking, isn't she?' Sam remarked. 'I'm pleased she's not my boss though.' She didn't recognise anyone else. 'No celebs then? I was hoping for Brad Pitt, at least.'

'I think that's him now,' Dom said straight faced and looking up at a helicopter beginning to circle overhead.

Sam looked at him warily. 'You are pulling my leg aren't you?'

Dom raised an eyebrow, 'well, you'll find out soon enough.' He looked Sam up and down, causing her to look flustered, 'I hear Brad likes his girls with long hair though.' Before she could answer, he moved away to shake hands with someone he recognised.

Sam found herself alone, wondering whether he was serious about Brad Pitt. Then she remembered it was a television event. Brad was an A grade celeb. He'd never stoop to a TV thing about the Tudors, would he? Then she had another thought. What if he's a financial backer?

***

'I nearly wet myself,' Sam said, talking over peals of laughter coming from Anne and Dom. 'It was so unfair,' she jabbed an accusing finger at Dom.

'You actually believed me?' Dom said incredulously.

Anne tried to rescue her friend. 'Well, I saw him crossing the field from that helicopter, and from a distance he did look Brad Pittish.'

Sam looked sorry for herself. 'Thank you, Annie,' she pouted, 'he did look Pittish, didn't he?'

The three were sitting together on a low garden wall, sipping Pimms. Anne looked over to Millie, who was sitting cross-legged on the other side of the garden. It took a moment for Anne to realise that she was talking to someone. 'Who is Millie nattering away to?'

Millie sat amongst plants and hedges; it was hard to see.

All three of them looked in the direction, trying to work out the answer. It was a warm, tranquil afternoon, the Pimms had taken effect and no one was troubled.

Anne stood up and called Millie.

Millie half-turned, gave Anne a quick wave, and turned back.

'Whoever it is, is more interesting than you,' Sam said.

Anne began to walk slowly towards Millie. 'I need to be nosey,' she said.

When Anne was out of earshot, Dom asked how Sam was doing. He knew the library had formally closed its doors and she was out of a job. 'Well, my last pay arrives next week. I've got a bit put by, but I really need to stop feeling sorry for myself and get a job. God knows where, and what.'

Dom felt out of his depth. There was nothing he could say or do to make her feel better. He reached down and gave her hand a squeeze. Any other time he'd expect a saucy remark, but today she sat quietly, watching Anne walk back with Millie.

'Hello nuisance,' Dom said as Millie approached.

Millie gave him a parp on her clown horn.

Sam sounded melancholy: 'Sums things up nicely.'

Anne turned around and appeared to be looking for someone.

'Who was it?' Dom asked, assuming she was seeking the person Millie had spoken to.

Millie picked up the thread. 'She's the quiet lady,' she said. She raised her hands over her head. 'And she has a big bun of hair on the top of her head, with a ribbon.'

Dom felt the hairs stand up on his forearms. He was about to say something when Sam intervened.

'What was she wearing, Millie?'

'A long, long dress and a big belt.'

'Well, I can't see anyone who looks like that,' Anne said, continuing to look around.

Dom nudged Sam. 'She's gone to her car probably,' Dom suggested, 'people are coming and going all the time.'

'Are they?' Anne sounded doubtful.

Sam tried to steer the conversation. 'Do they serve ice cream at this event, Dom?'

Millie jumped up and down as Dom pointed to a small cart staffed by a man in a boater hat. She pulled Anne off in his direction.

'It had to be Alice, didn't it?' Sam said, once Anne had gone.

'Certainly sounded like her, but it doesn't fit the pattern. Millie isn't grieving for anyone.'

Sam nodded thoughtfully. 'That's right.'

'But then you weren't certain about the date of your dad's death. Do you suppose young children can see her?'

Sam didn't answer. She simply didn't know. 'Well, one thing I'm sure of is that I'll have time on my hands soon enough. I'll see what I can dig up about the Colby family. Maybe that story Harry told us offers a thread.'

India Morley reappeared. She drew heavily on a cigarette and stood sizing up the pair of them. 'You two look like you're up to no good,' she said, raising a mischievous eyebrow.

'And you are smoking again,' Dom answered critically.

India tossed her head back. 'I can't do rural and no smoking in the same day. It's too much to tolerate.' She looked over Sam. 'Are you a writer, my dear?'

'I am a mere servant of them,' Sam answered.

'She's a librarian,' Dom added.

'Ex,' Sam corrected. 'I'm on the scrapheap with all the other librarians that local Councils no longer wish to employ.'

India inclined her head to one side. 'Are you two -?' She pointed her cigarette from one to the other.

'No, we're not,' Dom said. He drained his glass.

India was more astute. She looked at Sam's reaction to her question then said, 'perhaps.' She dropped her cigarette and stepped on it with her Louboutin stiletto. 'Dom, can we have a few moments alone please.'

***

'So you see, you'll be away for several months, once you tot everything up.' India reached for another cigarette. 'And before you complain, let me remind you this is all in the contract you clearly never bothered to read.'

Dom felt dejected. He was now expected to go to America and be available while the television series was being put together. His contract specified appearances on shows, talks, presentations and book signings. In short, everything he disliked. It was the double-edged sword of literary success. These days there was no such thing as just being able to write a good book, it spun off in all directions, and it felt like he was expected to be available at all of them.

India patted his knee. 'Cheer up, dear boy. You know what they say, anticipation is always the worst part.' She stood up, enveloped in a cloud of smoke and Chanel. 'Well, I have places to be. My staff will contact you with the full itinerary. You'd best pack your case and be ready to move in two weeks.' Her heels clacked their way to the door. 'Lovely kitchen,' she said insincerely.

She was on the edge of departing, when Dom had an idea. He knew India wanted to keep him sweet, so if anyone had the resources and could pull this together, she could. It was time to get something out of this that he wanted.

20 BURNKEY VILLAGE

Sam checked the documents again. So far as she could tell, the last direct descendant of the Colby family lived in a village just three miles away. Her name was Linda Colby. As to whether anyone in the current generation would know about the school fire was another thing altogether. They were also making a huge assumption that Colby, the convicted arsonist, caused the school fire. He may have begun his fire setting only *after* seeing the school go up in flames. It would have made quite an impression on a young mind. The real culprit could still be Alice Drew's father.

They might also misunderstand why Alice Drew haunted the Old School House. There were at least two sides to this. Until recently, it had been assumed that grief in the living was key to seeing Alice. But little Millie's description of the quiet lady at Dom's party sounded very much like her and undermined the assumption. Then of course was the reason why she continued to haunt the Old School House. Again, their assumptions related to unfinished business, of the need to correct some injustice, but what if they were wrong? Harry Wells had said something about us potentially being surrounded by spirits but not even knowing it. What if some of them simply shared the same space? Perhaps she and Dom were looking for answers to the unanswerable.

Still, it was a potential lead and one Dom would no doubt be pleased to follow up. If it came to nothing, there was surely no harm in trying.

Knowledge of Alice Drew also appeared to give comfort to Harry Wells. No doubt they would learn more about his situation in time.

It was mid-morning and Sam was still in bed, surrounded by documents. She was jobless, but had decided a couple of weeks of doing nothing added up to a well-deserved break. Once she contacted Dom about her findings she could go online and begin job searching.

She realised she'd been thinking a lot about Dom recently. Despite her attempt to give space to Anne, nothing had happened. Even if he did have designs on Anne, her natural reserve might be interpreted as indifference, which could be off-putting.

Maybe she just needed to talk to Anne again? Maybe something was happening in the background she was unaware of? She didn't want to compete with her friend and she certainly didn't want to lose her friendship.

Plus of course, Dom may have no interest in her that way. If he did, maybe he'd toss her to one side once the fun was over. She'd had enough of those times, but after the death of his wife he might view a fling simply as a way of getting back in the saddle?

It was all if's, but's and maybe's.

She shook her head, to clear it. It was time to get up and have a shower.

After a forty-minute search, through boxes, Dom finally uncovered his passport. He was relieved to see it was still in date. He had exactly two weeks before his servitude to the television company began. Even now, he imagined India sitting in her office, piling on the appointments and liaising with TV executives in order to squeeze more airtime for him.

He picked up his photo of Alice and looked at it, thinking he mustn't forget to take it. And then he felt a surge of guilt. To his shame he realised he'd been thinking about Sam while still looking at Alice.

He gently repositioned the frame. He could hear Alice saying, *she's lovely, just get on with it, you're wasting your life.* Or maybe he was just trying to lessen his guilt by thinking that.

His phone trilled into life. 'Hi Sam, just been thinking about you.'

'Me too,' Sam replied. Her normal banter eluded her, so she got to the point. 'I've found what I believe to be the last living relative of the Colby family.'

'That's fantastic,' Dom said excitedly. 'Don't tell me, he or she lives in Bolivia.'

'It's a she, and she lives in the village of Burnkey.'

'But that's almost next-door. Shall we pay her a visit?'

Sam relayed the thoughts she'd been having earlier. It had a sobering effect on the conversation.

'With all that's been going on I haven't really been focusing properly,' Dom said. 'Even so, I can't see what we've got to lose.'

'What about Harry Wells.'

Dom grimaced. In a moment of largesse, he'd promised Harry continued involvement, but now he was less sure. 'What do we do with him?'

'Maybe just say where we're up to. He might decide there's nothing for him to do.'

'True enough.'

'Look, if you're busy, I'll give him a call and we can both pop over to Burnkey this afternoon, after lunch.' They agreed a time and place to meet and Dom hung up.

He checked his emails. There was one from India Morley saying she'd managed to pull a few people together and it was looking good. He felt excited. He loved giving surprises and this one, he hoped, would be mind blowing.

***

'That's it over there,' Sam said. They were sitting in Dom's old Volvo, studying a row of terraced cottages.

'Well we don't want to frighten the poor woman. Maybe I should go alone,' Dom suggested.

'Woman to woman would be better, I think. Why don't you stay here and I'll explain you're researching local history for a new book? If it goes alright, I'll give you a wave.'

Dom nodded his approval. 'I'm pleased you spoke to Harry,' he said. 'If what he says is true, any confession, if we can call it that, needs to be done where Miss Drew can hear it.'

'Step at a time,' Sam said. 'Let's just see if Linda Colby is amenable. If she is, you may need to offer some incentive.' She rubbed her fingers together, signifying cash.

Dom rolled his eyes. 'Why am I not surprised?'

The village seemed deserted as Sam crossed the road. She went straight to the door and rang the bell. A small dog started yapping. Moments later she could hear a chain being slid back. The door opened. She went pale and took a step back. 'Kenny,' she exclaimed.

Kenny looked equally perplexed. His paranoid reaction was to look up and down the street, before locking eyes on Sam.

Sam caught the pungent smell of skunk on him. She pulled herself around. 'Stone me,' she said.

'Yeah, funny,' Kenny said. He had a stream of questions: 'What do you want? How did you know I was here? Who put you up to it?'

'I'm here to see Linda, not you,' Sam said, sounding more confident than she felt. There was an aggressive edge to Kenny that made her feel vulnerable.

Kenny looked her up and down. 'She's out.'

'Any idea when she'll be back?'

He began closing the door and spotted the Volvo across the road. 'Is he with you? What's he want?'

Sam sighed. 'It's not about you, Kenny. We'd like to speak to Linda.'

Kenny had renewed interest. 'What about?'

'It's private.'

Sam's comment only served to peak Kenny's interest more. He studied the man in the Volvo more carefully. 'I've seen him somewhere,' he said. He quickly gave up trying to recall. 'Are you and him at it then?'

She ignored the question and turned it back on Kenny. 'So are you and Linda living together?'

He resorted to type. 'I've got things to do,' he said, then slammed the door in her face.

As Sam crossed the road back to the car she could feel herself shaking from adrenaline. How was she going to explain this to Dom, she wondered?

'That went well,' Dom said, as she slid onto the passenger seat. He caught Sam's expression.

'Are you alright? What did he say to you?' He made ready to get out of the car.

Sam put her hand on his arm to stop him. 'He lives with Linda Colby,' she said hesitantly, 'and, we've got history.'

'History?'

'You know.'

Dom was taken aback. 'You and him?'

'It was a long time ago and it meant nothing,' she said. She looked at Dom pleadingly and gripped his arm. 'Please don't say anything to Anne about what I just said.'

He felt confused. 'Of course, if you don't want me to.'

'I mean it Dom. That's also Millie's dad.'

It fell into place. 'Oh, I see.'

Sam felt compelled to fill in the blanks. When she finished she wondered if she'd just ruined any possible chance with Dom. He was looking straight ahead, expressionless. 'Are you going to say something?'

They exchanged glances before he continued looking straight ahead. 'Well, as you say, it was a long time ago. But you mustn't worry, my lips are sealed.' He turned over the engine and pulled away.

They had gone about a mile when Sam asked him to pull over.

He found a quiet spot and brought the car to a halt. 'I know what you're thinking,' he said, 'have we ground to a halt so far as Alice Drew is concerned?' He shook his head. 'It really doesn't matter,' he said.

'Actually, that's not what I was thinking,' Sam said cautiously. She turned towards him. 'I don't want to pussyfoot around any more. I just need to know if you have any feelings for me?' She looked down and started to gabble. 'Look, I understand perfectly if you and Anne have something going on and I'd love it if she was happy, only I just don't know and what with Kenny just now, I wonder whether . .' She felt his fingertips against her cheek and stopped talking. When their eyes met he was looking back at her with some curious mixture of pity and need. He smiled sadly. 'I do,' he said. 'I mean, I think I have been developing feelings for you, but there's something I need to tell you.'

Sam felt herself droop. 'Oh God, you're gay, or you're a bigamist.'

'I'm leaving.'

Sam was stunned. 'Leaving,' she repeated. Her head was spinning. 'But I thought you loved it here?'

'I do and it's not forever. I want to come back.'

'Well, how long is not forever?'

'Months, maybe a year. I don't know. It's out of my hands.' He reached over and took her hand. 'The thing is, Sam, I'm a relationships man. I just feel it would be wrong to start something and then walk away.'

Sam took offence. 'Oh that's what *you* feel is it?'

He looked offended by her reaction. 'Yes, I think it is.'

She glared at him then opened the car door. She struggled to maintain her composure. 'The thing about relationships, as I understand them, is that two people are involved in decision making.'

'But we're not in a relationship, Sam,' he answered. He watched as she got out of the car. 'What are you doing?'

She leaned in. 'What do you think we've been in, these past weeks, Dominic? You think the fact that we haven't slept together means we're not in a relationship? You think I haven't been affected by the news you've just imparted, because of how you choose to define a relationship?' You're utterly selfish. She snorted and slammed the door shut.

Dom jumped out and began calling to her back. 'Sam, please. I'm sorry. Get back in the car and I'll drive us back. We can talk properly.'

He drove home alone.

21 A MESSAGE

Dom once heard that people are less suspicious of someone sitting in the passenger seat of a car than they are of a driver. It was a trick used by private detectives who needed to sit and watch for lengthy periods of time, but not drawing attention to themselves. People just figured they were waiting for the driver to return. He parked at the end of the road, changed seats and settled in for a long wait.

After just thirty minutes his patience was rewarded. He got out of the car and followed the woman who he took to be Linda Colby. She cleared the end of the road and he caught up. 'Miss Colby?' he asked.

She was young, timid looking and scrawny. Her hair was lank and in need of a wash.

'Who's asking?' She looked him over warily. 'You police?' The accent was London.

He took half a step back, not wanting to intimidate her and raised his hands. 'Not police, I promise. I'm actually a writer and I've been looking into local history.'

She scanned her surroundings suspiciously. 'Did your mate come round the other day?'

There was no point in lying. 'Sam, yes she did.'

She crossed her arms defiantly. 'I heard about that. So, what do you want, I haven't got all day?'

He could feel the potential for progress ebbing away. 'I'm interested in what you might know about your ancestors. I'm simply following up leads on families that have lived in the same area for generations. I believe you may be the last of the Colby line.'

She gave him a hard stare. 'How would you know that? You been prying into my business?' She began scratching the inside of her arm.

Dom noticed what he took to be track marks from injections. This wasn't looking good. 'Not at all,' he protested, 'these are public records. Anyone can look them up.'

She seemed to accept his response. She began to look uncomfortable and clearly wanted to get away. 'Look, I don't know anything, alright.' She turned and began to walk briskly in the direction of a bus stop. He could see a man waiting, looking furtively at the pair of them; maybe her supplier. It felt like a dead end for his enquiry and time to draw a line.

Dom returned home and began to pack. He kept thinking about Sam, wondering if she had calmed down and whether he should call. Two days had passed since she stormed off. He began to wonder if there was something missing from the male brain. Within the space of a few moments they had declared feelings for one another. Then, as a result of his honesty, she had given him a mouthful about relationships and gone off in a huge sulk. How could she say they were in a relationship? Surely it was a friendship? They were different things, weren't they?

As he continued to mull over the intricacies and complexities of the human condition, the doorbell rang. His hopes that it might be Sam were dashed. Harry Wells stood there, laden with bags, looking hopeful. 'Sam told me you'd tracked down a Colby,' he said expectantly. 'Now, I know you might have views about equipment, but this is only for my benefit. I promise that any data I gather will not be shared, unless I get your prior approval.'

Dom took a step back to allow Harry in. As he eased his way through the doorway, Dom began his apology.

'So, she's not coming over?' Harry sounded deflated.

'I think if you'd met her, you'd see why.'

Harry slumped in a seat and looked around. He spotted a couple of suitcases. 'Going somewhere?'

'Soon. I have to ship over to the States for a while.'

'Very nice,' Harry said, sounding impressed. 'So is the place empty while you're away?'

'Not if things go to plan,' Dom said vaguely, 'I'm just waiting for a friend to call.'

'Well, would you mind if I set up this recording equipment? It can go anywhere; it's battery operated.' Harry held up a small case.

Dom shrugged: Harry and his paranormal equipment. Still, it was the least he could do in the circumstances. 'Sure, where would you like to put it?'

Harry pointed to the top of the piano. 'Is that alright?'

'Fine. What does it record?'

Harry was about to answer when the doorbell rang.

'Again?' Dom said. 'I wonder if that's Sam?'

He opened the door expectantly only to be confronted by Kenny King and Linda Colby.

'Linda,' he said, sounding surprised. He fancied she had acquired a bruise to her right cheek since the last time her saw her. He looked critically at Kenny.

Kenny sniffed: 'I knew I'd seen you somewhere. You were in the paper with my Sam. You're that writer.'

Dom pulled in his chin with disbelief. '*My* Sam? I'm not sure she sees it that way.'

Linda scowled at Kenny, which only served to feed his cocky attitude.

'How much?' Kenny asked. He nodded towards Linda.

Dom spoke directly to Linda. 'If you'd like to come in for a chat, you're most welcome. As for payment, we can discuss that inside.'

'No,' Kenny said stridently. 'First, the payment.'

'I wasn't expecting you,' Dom said, still talking to Linda. 'I've only got– ,' he pulled out his wallet and flashed fifteen pounds.

'That'll do,' Kenny said.

Dom passed it to Linda.

'Give it him,' Linda said.

Dom reluctantly put the cash Kenny's way.

'I'll be back in a bit,' Kenny said. He strutted off, leaving Linda squirming with discomfort.

'You'd better come in,' Dom said.

Linda followed him in. Dom introduced Harry to her. He could see that Harry made the connection. Harry said he'd wait outside while they had their chat.

'We won't be that long,' Linda said, imposing a time limit.

'Take a seat,' Dom said.

She sat on the edge of the seat nearest her, looking tense. 'Got a fag?' she asked.

Dom said he didn't smoke. He watched as she resigned herself to the fact. She turned down the offer of a drink, saying Kenny wouldn't be long.

Dom sat at a comfortable distance from her. 'It is just a chat, Linda,' he said reassuringly.

She looked about her. Dom had the uneasy feeling she was making a mental inventory of the contents.

'Go on then,' she said impatiently.

Dom reached for his notepad. 'Well, as I think you already know, you seem to be the last of the Colby line in your family.'

As he spoke their attention was drawn to a sheet of music drifting down from the piano.

'Just a draught,' Dom said uneasily. He was suddenly aware of the fact that Alice Drew might have other ideas about Linda Colby should be treated. He refocused. 'A long time ago there was a fire in this very building, when it was a school.'

'Everyone knows that,' Linda answered.

'Good,' Dom said supportively. 'Now, all I'm trying to do is get to the bottom of how it started.'

Linda pulled a face. 'Bit late for that isn't it?'

'You're probably right,' Dom answered casually. 'It's just I've heard two different stories and I wondered if you might be able to help?'

The tension seemed to leave Linda's body as she realised he really was no threat. She said nothing but Dom thought he detected just a glimmer of something in her eye.

He briefly related the two versions of the story but was at pains to sound indifferent to the outcome. He wrapped up with, 'anyway, as you say, it was a long time ago.'

She sat tight-lipped for a moment and then made a decision. Maybe it had been a long time since anyone had shown interest in her? Whatever the reason, she decided to talk to Dom. 'Grandma used to say it was our Frank, he was a bad 'un by all counts.'

A humming noise came from the piano, like wind blowing through the base strings. Linda frowned and turned her attention to the source.

Dom felt uneasy and began to wonder what might be in store. He quickly spotted Harry's recording device on top of the piano, which gave him an idea. 'Don't worry about the noise, it's that thing.' He waggled a finger.

'What is it?' Linda asked.

Dom had an idea. 'It detects dampness inside the piano.' The moment it passed his lips he thought, what an idiot.

She looked blank. Dom pressed on before she could start asking more questions.

'In what way was he bad?'

Since the interruption, she was less interested in feeding his curiosity. 'Dunno.'

There was a banging on the door. Linda sprang to her feet. Sounding relieved, she said it would be Kenny.

Dom opened up and sure enough, there he stood, with two recently acquired packets of cigarettes in his hand. He passed a cigarette to Linda, who almost snatched in from his fingers.

'If you want more, you'll have to pay more,' Kenny said slyly.

'You're quite the business manager, aren't you,' Dom's comment dripped with contempt.

Kenny wasn't sure how to take it. He sniffed, stood for a moment to give Dom another chance, then turned away.

As they walked off he heard Kenny berate Linda for not using the opportunity to invent more stories.

Dom closed the door, pleased to see the back of them.

Harry emerged from the kitchen. 'That was interesting.'

'What there was of it,' Dom said. 'Still no definitive proof that Frank Colby was the culprit. And even if Linda said it was him, it doesn't actually prove it.'

Harry was tinkering with his equipment. 'There's some interesting stuff going on here,' he said distractedly. 'I need to process this.' He secured the lid and pulled it off the piano.

'Thought you were leaving it here?'

Harry had a strange look on his face. 'Not sure it'll get much better than this,' he said.

As Dom let Harry out the door, the telephone rang.

One of those days, Dom thought. It was India Morley, telling him everything was set.

'Are you quite sure?' India asked.

'Well, it's worth a try,' Dom answered.

He felt unsettled. Maybe it was Sam, or seeing Linda with that idiot of a boyfriend, or getting ready to travel. He wandered around the house picking things up and moving them around.

He suddenly felt very alone. He picked up the photograph of Alice. He imagined her saying, *don't indulge it, go and do something*.

So, he tried to keep himself busy and decided to check on the barn. He stepped inside and looked over the containers of books. Nothing had changed, but he smiled at the prospect of what he hoped was about to come.

As he turned to leave, a gust of wind blew in. One of the books nearby flapped open and a sheet blew out. He picked it up and looked at it. It was a poem by someone called Harry Scott-Holland:

Death is nothing at all.
It does not count.
I have only slipped away into the next room.
Nothing has happened.

Everything remains exactly as it was.
I am I, and you are you,
and the old life that we lived so fondly together is untouched, unchanged.
Whatever we were to each other, that we are still.

Call me by the old familiar name.
Speak of me in the easy way which you always used.
Put no difference into your tone.
Wear no forced air of solemnity or sorrow.

Laugh as we always laughed at the little jokes that we enjoyed together.
Play, smile, think of me, pray for me.
Let my name be ever the household word that it always was.
Let it be spoken without an effort, without the ghost of a shadow upon it.

Life means all that it ever meant.
It is the same as it ever was.
There is absolute and unbroken continuity.
What is this death but a negligible accident?

Why should I be out of mind because I am out of sight?
I am but waiting for you, for an interval,
somewhere very near,
just round the corner.

All is well.
Nothing is hurt; nothing is lost.
One brief moment and all will be as it was before.
How we shall laugh at the trouble of parting when we meet again!

Tears formed in his eyes and his chest heaved. He held his breath for a moment then slowly breathed out. Was this a coincidence? No, he'd given up on those.
Finally, she had been able to send him a message and it was simple: so very Alice.

22 TEA AND TRACES

The local job search had drawn a blank. Anything worth applying for was at least twenty miles away. Sam began to consider if she'd need to sell her cottage and move to where the work was. She slapped the lid of her laptop shut and wondered if it was too early to crack open a bottle of wine. Perhaps the decent thing to do was get out of her pyjama's first.

Then she thought about Dom – again. Had she been completely unreasonable? Why hadn't he contacted her? She wished she didn't have such a short fuse. Her mother always said it would get her into trouble, but she doubted if this was the sort of thing she had in mind. She went back over the memories again. He had feelings for her; wasn't that what she wanted to know? He was leaving, but then he said he was coming back.
She decided it was time to swallow her pride and get back in contact.

The letterbox clattered. She scooped up the delivery, kept hold of the envelopes and threw the pamphlets to one side. One immediately caught her eye. It was obviously a high quality, heavy white weave, with a crest she didn't recognise. She sat at the kitchen table and took out the contents. The paper bent like parchment. On the top it said: *From the Desk of India Morley*. She remembered her from Dom's party.

She read it twice but still couldn't fathom if it meant what she thought it meant. She grabbed the phone and called Dom. He picked up almost immediately.

'Sam, I'm so pleased you called. Have you forgiven me yet?'
She wasn't sure if he sounded pitifully sincere or just pitiful.
'I'm edging in that direction,' she said, a smile playing on her lips.
'It's my boyish charm, isn't it? It's hard to stay angry with me. But
honestly, if you hadn't phoned, I'd have been beating your door down in
a couple of hours.'
'Well then, I've saved you the cost of a new door.'
'Can we meet? There's a few things I need to say.'
'Sure. But first, I've just received a letter from this India Morley person.
She seems to be asking me to set up a book shop at your place.'
'Ah, she's beaten me to it,' Dom said. 'I wanted to say something sooner
but,' he paused, trying to find the right words, 'but with the way we left
things, the opportunity didn't arise.'
'Well I'm all ears now,' Sam replied.

They met for lunch at the pub.
'You look nice,' Dom said.
Sam had made an effort with clothing and makeup but played it down.
'You've noticed, finally.' She immediately felt she'd been too harsh. She
backtracked. 'Thank you,' she smiled. She reached into her bag for the
letter and showed it to Dom.
He scanned it and nodded. 'Looks about right.' He looked up at her. 'If
this is what you want?'
'So, she's asking me to set up a book business for her? Where? In your
barn?'
Dom smiled. 'I'm not being very helpful am I? Because I'll be abroad for
a long time I asked India if she could get her business types involved. I
want to get the village library up and running again, but it'll just
flounder again unless we diversify. What this is saying,' he held up the
letter, 'is that a library can function alongside a book business. If you're
interested, you'll be the librarian, plus you'll run the online side of book
sales.'

Sam looked overwhelmed. 'You've done all this for me?' She shook her
head trying to absorb it all. All she could think to say was, 'it'll take a
while to knock the barn into shape.'
'Oh, help is on it's way,' Dom said. India is sending her design crew and
business guru this way. It's probably best to stand back and let them do
their thing. And it's not the barn, it's the house. I'm giving over the Old
School House to be the library.'

Sam looked at him with sad eyes. 'So you're really not coming back?'
He reached across the table and took her hands. 'Ah, but I am. I'll
certainly be back for Christmas, and again when I get breaks in the
schedule. One day it has to come to an end.' He gave her hands a
squeeze. 'This is my home now, Sam. I'll be back, only I think it's time
for a fresh start. It'll be good to give the Old School House back as a
place of learning.'
'You're thinking of Alice Drew, aren't you?'
He nodded. 'Partly, yes. And myself. Oh, and there are things I need to
update you in that regard involving Linda Colby.'
She looked startled.
'Don't worry, it's all done and dusted. Suffice to say that I think the
cause of the fire will remain something of a mystery.'
'And Alice Drew?'
Dom inclined his head to one side. 'I've no idea. Perhaps she's content.
The one stipulation I've made is that the piano stays. If Alice chooses to,
or if she even has a choice, there's music and books to keep her
company.'

The landlord delivered two ploughman's lunches to their table. When
he moved out of earshot, Sam leaned forward and whispered: 'and
what about us?'
Dom looked at her cautiously. 'As you say, we're already in a
relationship.'
Sam thought he was being evasive. 'I think you know what I mean,
Dom.'
He sighed with exasperation. 'I don't know how to answer you, Sam. I'm
going away in just a few days. I don't want anyone hurt, me or you. It's
early days and if we still feel the same when I get back, we'll know for
sure.'

Sam's expression hardened. She stood up. 'Come with me.'
What have I said this time, Dom thought. He looked at their meals.
Sam called over to the Landlord. 'Geoff, put these on my tab. We've
remembered something, sorry.' She spun around and headed out of the
door.
Dom picked up his jacket and followed her.
As he stepped onto the street, she threw her arms around his neck and
kissed him. When they came up for air she told him he was over

cautious, over concerned and life was just too short. 'You're coming back to my place and we're making use of the time we have before you go.'

It had been a while, but once more he found himself doing what he was told, and enjoying every moment of it.

***

'Yes, he's with me now,' Sam said. She looked over at Dom, sprawled naked, face down on her bed and fast asleep. 'Well, he's been quite busy,' she said smiling, 'but I'm sure he'd like to meet with you Harry. What time?'

Dom shifted onto his side and cracked open an eye.

'I'll let him know. If there's a problem I'm sure he'll get back to you.' She hung up.

'Harry Wells,' Dom croaked. 'What have you signed me up for?'

She jumped on the bed and sat astride him. 'I'll tell you for a price,' she giggled.

He moaned playfully: 'I can't. There's nothing left of me.'

She looked into his eyes. 'Now, isn't this better than a ploughman's lunch?'

He put his hands behind his head and sounded serious. 'That ploughman's had a fine Stilton cheese with it. I feel robbed.'

She looked thoughtful. 'What you need, Mr Ross, is some distraction.'

***

That evening Harry Wells turned up with some different equipment. Dom and Sam were waiting for him at the Old School House.

'Wait until you see what I've got,' he said. He unravelled a scroll of paper and set up a couple of audio speakers. He sat opposite Dom and Sam, his elbows on his knees, his hands expansive. 'The audio has different layers,' he explained. 'It's easier if we do this in stages.' He placed a chubby finger over one of the buttons. 'The first audio is the conversation you had with Linda Colby. Thankfully I had the presence of mind to switch the kit on as soon as you introduced us.' He played the audio.

'So that's what you neglected to tell me,' Sam said to Dom. 'Didn't seem to get very far though.'

'Now,' Harry said, I'll play it again but with this second layer overlapping. Just listen.'

They strained. At first, all they could hear was hissing that served to blur what Linda was saying. Then a whooshing sound came and went.

'Catch that?' Harry asked.

They nodded.

'Right, now I'll remove the audio of Linda altogether. This is recorded at a much higher frequency, which I've reduced so that we can hear it.'

Dom could feel himself becoming tense. What started out as a way of indulging Harry had suddenly become serious. He felt Sam's clammy hand grab his.

The hissing returned, then they heard it, a single audible word: *liar*

'Jesus,' Sam gasped. 'What the hell was that?'

Harry pointed to the scroll of paper he'd unravelled. 'It corresponds exactly to this,' he said. 'It's a very slight fluctuation in room temperature.' He grinned mischievously, 'What you might think of as a disturbance in the force.'

'But what does it mean?' Dom asked.

'It corroborates the speech pattern. It happens at exactly the same time. You couldn't fake this.'

Dom and Sam exchanged glances.

'I'm not so sure I fancy working here,' Sam said.

Harry looked at them both. 'I thought I'd just let that part sink in. But there's more.'

Sam covered her mouth. 'Is this going to freak us out, Harry?

'Well I just think it's fascinating,' he said. 'These aren't super beings. They're just the echo of ordinary people, like you and me.' He waited for a response.

Dom raised his eyebrows. 'Lead on then, Mr Wells.'

They went through the same process, but this time the audio lasted longer. All Dom and Sam could hear was white noise, punctuated with the occasional blip. Harry switched off.

'I know what you're thinking,' he said. 'You didn't hear another voice. At first I couldn't work out the recordings, but then it struck me.' He pulled open the scroll a bit further. A red a green line intersected at points and then gradually subsided in parallel.

'There are two of them,' he announced, 'talking to one another.'

Dom could feel his eyes widen as a chill ran down his spine.

Sam voiced how she felt. 'I think I might puke.'

'Well, what do you think it means, Harry?' Dom asked.

Harry nodded slowly. 'If you want my honest opinion, I think the first person has been calmed down by the second.' He drew their attention back to the trace. 'This is the first person. The trace is getting higher and this can be associated with an increased likelihood in paranormal activity. It's like someone chucking a cup at the wall out of sheer frustration. But before it gets to that point, there's a kind of intervention, for want of a better word. He or she has been calmed down before it goes to far. And look,' his finger followed the trace as is gradually reduced and flat-lined. 'I think they've gone.'

'For good?' Sam asked.

'Who knows,' Harry answered.

'Two people,' Dom repeated. 'Miss Drew and her father perhaps?' He scratched his head. 'I wonder,' he muttered to himself.

'What are you thinking?' Sam rubbed her hands anxiously and stood up. 'It just feels so weird occupying the same space as spirit people.'

'It's an honour,' Harry said. 'It's all about perspective. This has to be the most active property on the planet. It's just a damn shame we're keeping it to ourselves. Can you imagine the effect on the scientific community, not to mention the church?'

'But you just said they've gone,' Sam said. 'What if we spilled the beans and they really have gone. We'd look a right bunch.'

They paused for thought.

'I have an idea,' Dom said. I'm making some tea.'

23 THE BIG REVEAL

The nasal tones of the floor manager filled the studio. 'That's all for now, everyone. Have a good Christmas.' The studio gave up a collective whoop. Some rushed for the door, others targeted the drinks table. 'Staying for the party?' asked India. Despite the fact they were in a studio she was wearing large sunglasses. Her cigarette dangled from the end of a jade holder. The effect was 1930s movie diva, but in these surroundings it was barely noticeable.

'Can't,' Dom said, checking his watch. 'I've got a flight to catch and I need to pack.'

India smiled. 'It's the girl I met at your garden party, isn't it? The one we've been working with to salvage that strange little library.'

Dom gathered up his notes from the floor. 'What's strange about it?'

India shook her head dismissively. She regarded the whole enterprise as a boy's hobby. She changed subject. 'I'm thinking of moving here you know.'

Dom looked surprised. 'You're thinking of relocating to the States?'

She pouted. 'Maybe an office. It'll give me an excuse to move between the two.'

'I don't see why you need an excuse,' Dom said, stuffing the last of the papers in his bag.

She flicked ash from her cigarette. 'You would if you saw my annual tax demand,' she said. 'Which reminds me, I must give you the name of my accountant, you'll need him.'

He doubted it. He leaned in and kissed her on the cheek. 'Have a lovely Christmas.'

Dom arrived at the airport only to discover flights were being delayed due to bad weather. The holiday season was in full swing and people poured through the doors. With nobody leaving, the place was congested. Increasingly irritable business types paced around making calls. Bored children ran around, squealing. Lines of people leaned against trolleys, or sat on the floor, like refuges waiting to be rescued. The flight departure board announced delays from top to bottom. He found a corner and wedged himself in. Maybe he'd be spending the holiday here after all. He pulled out his phone and considered calling Sam before remembering the time difference. He flipped the lid off his coffee cup and took a bite from his bagel. It was shaping up to be a long day.

***

Sam ran the back of her hand across her brow. It had taken a while but the place looked fantastic. The first four weeks had been spent with architects and builders. They were at pains to include her in the decision making, something she was sure Dom had a hand in. She loved every minute of it: learning about design, materials, lighting, and how best to use light and space. It didn't take too long for the Old School House to be transformed. The interior became a sweeping curve of book shelves over two levels.

Dom had specified the exterior of the building was to remain the same and the piano was to stay. The architect was happiest with the exterior because the large windows illuminated the place perfectly. She was less certain about the piano, but after some discussion and a few compromises, she worked around it. Only Sam knew the reason why Dom had insisted the piano remain.

Sam couldn't get the entire book stock on the new shelves, but it meant she could rotate with material still in the barn. As part of the specification, a new section had been constructed specifically for book sales. One of India Morley's people had calculated a way that the tourist trail might be drawn towards the village. He'd encouraged Sam to stock up on books and maps relating to walking, wildlife, tours, places to stay and so on. He'd also been to the pub and found a receptive audience with Geoff, the landlord, regarding appealing layouts. It was as if India Morley had adopted the village. She must really have an investment in Dom, Sam thought.

A covered walkway had been constructed between the house and barn. The barn had been divided up so that book stocks were in one part and a smart new coffee shop took pride of place. The smell of freshly brewed coffee wafted about the place. This was part of the promised employment package. Someone was being trained up as a barista. Two more would work the café and two part-timers would work alongside Sam in the library and bookshop. The village felt like life had been injected into it.

The plan was to have the official opening before Christmas and then close it down again until early Spring. The idea, Sam was told, was to showcase the place with all its twinkling lights and get some media attention. They would use the time that followed to do some work in the gardens, extending the patio and seating areas for visitors

The last job of the day for Sam was attaching the interior signage. The big exterior sign would be erected the next day. Sam pulled the tape off the box, examined the contents and went about the business of sticking signs on bookshelves.

The big day finally arrived. Hot mince pies, drinks and snacks were piled high in the new coffee shop.
Sam had invested in a new outfit. The woman in the shop told her a short skirt with cinched waist would give her height. That was fine, but Sam put on her heels for absolute certainty.
She checked her phone again. Dom's messages about flight delays were utterly depressing but they had at least stopped. She hoped that meant he was on his way.
She'd missed him more than she realised. Video calls and texts were all well and good, but she wanted him back in her arms, yesterday.

The main outer library sign was up, covered over with tarpaulin and ready for the big reveal. Local television was on standby and the press were taking pictures. India Morley had suggested, more in the way of a command, that Dom would do the opening ceremony. Additional media coverage, however minor, was always welcome she said.

Sam thought it was a great idea. It was, after all, Dom's old house and from what she could gather, he was going to be something of a celebrity, once the television series was aired.

She checked her watch, it was almost midday and people were already starting to arrive ready for the opening at 1 p.m. They were meant to wait outside until the place was officially opened, but it was freezing cold. Sam ushered them inside. They looked around admiringly as they drifted towards the café.

By 1 p.m. Dom still hadn't arrived. The television crew were getting twitchy although the gently swelling crowd appeared content to sample the free snacks and drinks and to browse the books. Sam had already rung up a few sales.

There was no contingency plan in place for Dom's absence. Should Sam open the place herself she wondered?

She spotted Anne and Millie and an idea came to mind.

By 1.30 p.m. everyone was outside, standing in front of the building. Sam stepped up and announced what most people already knew. Bad weather in the States was causing travel chaos and it looked like Dominic Ross had been caught up. 'However, we have a very special young lady with us today, who just happens to be the first member of the children's library.'

Anne shepherded Millie to the front.

Millie stood shyly in front of the crowd and took hold of the chord passed to her by Sam.

Sam asked the crowd to countdown from three and Millie gave a tug.

The thin tarpaulin sheet tumbled down. People clapped, camera's clicked, cell phones captured the moment.

Sam moved forward and looked up at the sign: *The Alice Drew Library.*

People reassembled inside. Christmas lights came to life to another round of applause. The photographer wanted some 'people shots.' Sam knelt by the Christmas tree and passed out presents to the children. The staff assembled around a Christmas cake in the shape of a book. They wore elf hats and grinned. Christmas music rang out from the newly installed speakers. Adults loosened up as the wine began to flow. Some started to dance.

Sam circulated. She alternated between laughing and joking and becoming earnest with those wishing to discuss the book selection. At some point she began to notice the numbers had dwindled. Parents had taken children home for supper and the free food and drink was all but used up.

The staff began looking at the clock. It was 7 p.m. Sam realised they had places to be and things to do. She raised her voice over the few remaining people and announced the library was to close. The building emptied within moments.

She stood alone and looked about her. It had been a roaring success. The strains of Dean Martin singing *Let it Snow* filled the space. She wondered whether Alice Drew would approve. Having a library named after you surely counted for something.

She turned the music down, then the main lighting.

Her feet were throbbing. She kicked off her shoes and padded quietly towards the Christmas tree, searching for the plug to disconnect the lights.

A solitary mince pie caught her eye. She realised she was ravenous. She took a big bite and sighed as it melted in her mouth.

She became vaguely aware of cold air hitting the back of her neck. She turned, her mouth stuffed with mince pie, to see Dom standing in the doorway. Her heart missed a beat.

'Bit quieter than I'd hoped,' he quipped.

God he looked good, she thought. She stood and stared. His hair was too long and he hadn't shaved for a couple of days, but she could have eaten him where he stood. She collected herself and remembered her mouth was full. Their eyes met as she munched. It made Dom smile.

'Well, they heard you were coming,' she finally managed to get out. 'You seem to have this effect.'

He got the joke. He stepped into the library and looked around. 'I like it,' he said, dropping his shoulder bag to the floor.

'And?' she traced a finger across her eyebrow and playfully pursed her lips.

Dom came closer. 'And – I like you too.' They were very close when he stopped and looked up. 'Damn, no mistletoe.'

She grabbed his waist.

'Then you can't exercise your pagan rites,' Sam said sadly. 'However,' she reached across and plucked a small bauble from the tree, 'this ancient Norfolk kissing ritual only requires the presence of one of these.' She held it above his head as they pressed their body's together. He smelled of travel, coffee and cologne.

'There's so much more I have to learn about this place,' he said, softly tracing a fingertip across her cheek. 'Thankfully, I have time on my hands.'

24 TRUTH MATTERS

The television was on and hot snacks were about to be served. As best he could, Dom had explained to Millie what a Tudor was and why they wore funny clothes. He and Sam occupied the sofa while Millie sat on the floor between them.

Anne brought in a tray of drinks and told Millie the food was hot, so to be careful.

'It's so exciting,' Sam said, 'I mean, watching what you've written being brought to life.'

'Let's hope they do it justice,' Anne commented, as she curled up on a big soft chair with a plate of food.

Dom smiled and nodded, but he already new the answer. India had texted him hours earlier because the show had already aired in the States. The text said: *through the roof. kerching!* Yet more cash was coming their ways.

Episode one ran for forty minutes.

'Well, I'm gripped,' Anne said, as the credits rolled.

Millie asked if she could be a Tudor when she grew up.

Unusually for Sam she said nothing. She looked a little awestruck as she leaned in and kissed Dom on the cheek.

Millie said yuk, so Sam grabbed her and planted a big kiss on each cheek. The room filled with squeals and laughter.

Dom helped carry the plates into the kitchen. When he and Anne were alone, Anne confided she had never seen Sam so happy.

'She's besotted, you know.' She gave Dom a smile but there was a look of concern in her eyes.

He was happy to reassure her. 'Me too. I can't wait for all this to be done and dusted so that I can move back.'

Anne began stacking the plates. 'You won't miss the Hollywood lifestyle?'

'Not a bit. First and foremost, I'm a writer, I should be hiding in my Hobbit hole.' He looked over his shoulder to see Sam and Millie playing rough and tumble. 'Plus, I have a life I'd like to be getting on with. Still,' he sighed, 'my bank account has never been so healthy. I just wish-,' he went silent.

'You just wish Alice could have been here to enjoy it too?' Anne ventured.

He leaned against the sink. 'Something like that. But don't get the wrong idea, I wouldn't wish away what I have now.' He stepped to the sink and filled the kettle. 'So, what about you?'

'Same old,' Anne said. 'Just the way I like it really.'

He genuinely believed her. Anne was just one of those people who knew what they wanted and was content with her lot.

Sam joined them. 'Ah good, you're making coffee.'

Dom had put the kettle on and was looking out of the window. 'What do you know about that farm over there?'

Anne followed his line of sight. 'The one that's for sale? It's less of a farm and more a house with a 27 acre garden. The chap who owns it sold off most of the land. Why?'

Sam linked arms with him. 'He wants to be at one with the soil, don't you lad?'

'Got to hang my hat somewhere,' Dom said.

Anne watched as Sam's expression showed relief. Of late, many of their conversations related to Sam's concern over Dom being swept off his feet by some leggy actress. Anne was at pains to say he didn't seem the sort and now he was proving it. She knew Sam felt vulnerable. The new library, the fact that she and Dom were an item; it all felt too good. Sam was waiting for the bubble to burst.

Anne lined up the mugs for the coffee. 'So, how much longer will you be in the States?' She watched as he chewed his lower lip. Sam was studying his expression too.

'My guess is that India is fending off the requests for interviews.'
'Longer than you'd hoped then,' Sam said flatly.
He tried to brighten up. 'Maybe, but the series is on a roll, and I won't
be needed at the studio anymore.' He slid his arm over Sam's shoulder
and pulled her closer. 'It can't last forever and anyway they're talking
about commissioning another series.'
Sam pulled back with surprise. 'Another?'
He grinned. 'Maybe. But I have to write it first. Even India knows there's
a balance to be struck. I'll need plenty of me time,' he kissed the top of
her head, 'which means plenty of us time.'
Sam and Anne exchanged glances. Anne smiled encouragingly.
'Maybe we can all look around the farm,' Anne suggested.
Dom sounded enthused. 'Excellent idea. I'll arrange a time.'

***

Sam had saved front row seats for Harry Wells and Anne and the room
was packed. The Press had adopted Dom as a local writer and they now
hung on his every word.
Dom's big secret was closely guarded. Even Sam had no idea what his
presentation was about.

As Dom walked to the front the conversation in the room reduced to a
murmur and then silence. He casually introduced himself to the
audience. A polite ripple of applause followed.
Dom explained that the Old School House, where they were now
seated, had a history. He reminded the audience that his role as a writer
of historical fiction was to take what was known, and knit together the
unknown into the plausible.

He held up a small book. He said it was a short story he'd been working
on, based around the history of the building, its fire and the personal
sacrifice of Alice Drew. It described typical village life in the 1900s, the
way people lived, their beliefs and values. As to the fire itself, he
pointed to the darker side of idle speculation and finger pointing.
As an example, he mentioned the story Harry Well's had provided about
the little boy in the coal mine. He said such a wrong may well have
happened here, in the case of Alice Drew's father.

Injustice, he went on, was a heavy burden to carry. He hoped that by highlighting the story behind the Old School House, that fresh perspectives could be brought to light.

Dom then read from his book. There was no mention of ghosts beyond the story that most of the locals already knew of, but paid little attention to. He mixed facts with personal anecdotes and humour, keeping the audience entertained.

In his concluding statement, he said: 'if by any chance Miss Drew is listening, I would like her to know that we're fully aware of the very real possibility that her father was wrongly accused. Sitting here, over a century later, it's easy to think it no longer matters. But truth, as I'm sure you'll agree, always matters. I hope Miss Drew rests easy in the knowledge that another side to the story has finally been revealed. And, knowing her love of learning, I'm sure she would appreciate the use to which the Old School House has now been put.'

***

Sam and Anne stood in front of the newly purchased farm house.

'Think you'll like it here?' Anne asked.

'What's not to like,' Sam said. 'And he's given me a free hand to do the interior decorating. I was bragging about how much I'd picked up from the design team at the library.'

'Could be fun. What will you do with your cottage?'

'Rent it, maybe. We'll see.'

They strolled around the outside.

'Any plans for the land?'

'Yes,' Sam said. 'Dom says anything over an acre would send him mad. He wonders if you could use the rest for grazing, or growing carrots?'

'Seriously?'

'Seriously. He says if you're interested the price is for him to be kept in jersey milk and cream.'

Anne pushed her hands deep into her overall pockets and grinned. 'I'll fill his bath with the stuff once a week if he wants.'

The friends meandered about the place, speculating on possible uses for the few outbuildings.

Anne checked her watch. 'I'd better be getting off,' she said. 'Millie's going to a birthday party later and I need to get a present for her to take.'

'You're a good mum,' Sam said.

'And you're a good friend,' Anne replied.

They coupled arms and strolled back to Anne's car.

'He's made quite a difference to a lot of lives,' Anne said.

Sam agreed. 'Just to think, if you hadn't alerted Alice to the sale of the Old School House, none of this would be happening. I'd be jobless and I'd never have met Dom.

'Makes you wonder if someone has been looking over your shoulder,' Anne said.

'It really does,' Sam said, thoughtfully.

Sam stopped off at the Alice Drew library on her way home. She couldn't get enough of the place. She unlocked the door and walked around looking at the books. It induced in her a feeling of sheer pleasure.

On the way out she caught sight of copy of Dom's short story lying on the floor. She picked it up and looked at the title: *Miss Drew Remembered*. It had been bookmarked with a scrap of paper. She opened the book and found it marked at the point where Dom related his alternative views of what happened the fateful day of the fire. The scrap of paper fell to the floor. She picked it up and saw that something had been roughly pencilled on.

Thank you.

FROM THE AUTHOR

I very much hope you enjoyed the story. To find out what's new, or to contact me, please drop by my website jerrykennard.info

Other Books by Me:

AUGUSTUS REID (DECEASED)

BLACK POPPIES

SPITE

THE VIRION SCRIPT

17701668R00088

Printed in Great Britain
by Amazon